I0451501

ELLY HAYS

LORI CRANE

Lori Crane Entertainment, Inc.
www.LoriCrane.com

Cover design and formatting by Elite Book Design, LLC.

This book is a work of historical fiction. Some names, characters, places, and incidents are from historical accounts. Some names, characters, places, and incidents are products of the author's imagination.

ISBN: 978-0988354548
eBook ISBN: 978-0988354555

Muscogee Creek Indian Names

Muscogee Creek Indian names used in this story and their English translations:

Tafv Hokkolen (Two Feather)
    warrior of the Creek village

Nila (Victory)
    Tafv's wife

Hasse Ola (Rising Sun)
    Tafv and Nila's only son

Eto Lecv (Under the Tree)
    Tafv's brother

Mekko (Great Chief)
    Chief of the Creek village

Talisa (Beautiful Water)
    Mekko's granddaughter

Hillis Hiya (Medicine Man)
    public speaker for Mekko

TABLE OF CONTENTS

Tecumseh's Speech

The laborers had erected a small makeshift platform in the middle of the meadow. It rose two feet off the ground so Tecumseh could be seen above the massive gathering of people. Rumors had circulated for months that he would come, as it had been foretold by a bright comet in the nighttime sky in March of 1811, and the gathering crowd numbered into the hundreds, perhaps closer to a thousand, representing over a dozen of the twenty Mvskoke clans.

As the people waited for him to take the platform, they grew increasingly impatient. They had been assembling for days to hear him speak, so not only were they weary from their travels, but the scorching sun was not improving their disposition. The air was as stagnant as the wait, with not even the slightest of breezes to offer relief from the stifling heat. The afternoon sun melting into evening had made them agitated, and they grumbled and occasionally began chanting for the great warrior to appear and address them. When he did not take the platform after a few minutes, the chanting quieted to a dull objection, only to start up again within a short amount of time.

Over the last few months, reports had surfaced that the Americans would once again declare war against the British. Before and since the revolution, the British had befriended the Indians, asking for their help in warding off the Americans' expansion. Since the Indians considered the land theirs in the first place, they were pleased to oblige. The Indians had never asked for a favor in return, but the waves of white settlers were growing, continually trespassing upon their tribal land. They needed help, they needed answers, they needed to stop the encroachment. They eagerly awaited Tecumseh's speech and they were anxious to hear a plan. They wanted to know what he wanted of them. If the reports of an impending war were true, perhaps this was the time to join forces with the British and defeat the white man once and for all.

Finally, a group of elders dressed in vibrant tribal robes with headdresses embellished with porcupine fur and hawk feathers stepped up onto the platform. The cheer began small and grew to a fevered pitch as it spread across the field of warriors like a breeze washing over wheat. The elders greeted the crowd and led them in singing their tribal anthem, "Heleluyvn," following which the crowd erupted again in anticipation of the great warrior's arrival.

One of the village chiefs, dressed in a brown and white cape with fringe dangling from the bottom and glittering glass beads sewn into the edges, stepped forward and quieted the audience so he could make the introduction. "Braves and warriors, I give you Shawnee Chief Tecumseh!"

The crowd exploded in applause as the mighty warrior took center stage.

Tecumseh stood motionless on the platform, allowing the sun to shine on his face. He wore breechcloths, leather leggings, and a bright red coat. A large medallion hung around his neck, resting on his bare chest, and his hair was adorned with feathers, some standing straight up on his head, some hanging with his shoulder-length hair. After allowing a few minutes of adulation, Tecumseh raised his hands, gesturing for the crowd to quiet down. When he was confident everyone could hear him, he began.

"In defiance of the white warriors of Ohio and Kentucky, I have traveled through their settlements, once our favorite hunting grounds. No war-whoop was sounded, but there is blood on our knives. The Pale-faces felt the blow, but knew not whence it came. Accursed be the race that has seized on our country and made women of our warriors. Our fathers, from their tombs, reproach us as slaves and cowards. I hear them now in the wailing winds.

"The Muscogee was once a mighty people. The Georgians trembled at your war-whoop, and the maidens of my tribe, on the distant lakes, sung the prowess of your warriors and sighed for their embraces.

"Now, your very blood is white; your tomahawks have no edge; your bows and arrows were buried with your fathers. Oh! Muscogees, brethren of my mother, brush from your eyelids the sleep of slavery; once more strike for vengeance; once more for your country. The spirits of the mighty dead complain. Their tears drop from the weeping skies. Let the white race perish. They seize your land; they corrupt your women; they trample on the ashes of your dead!

"Back, whence they come, upon a trail of blood,

they must be driven. Back! Back, ay, into the great water whose accursed waves brought them to our shores! Burn their dwellings! Destroy their stock! Slay their wives and children! The Red Man owns the country, and the Pale-faces must never enjoy it.

"War now! War forever! War upon the living! War upon the dead! Dig their very corpses from the grave. Our country must give no rest to a white man's bones. This is the will of the Great Spirit, revealed to my brother, his familiar, the Prophet of the Lakes. He sends me to you. All the tribes of the north are dancing the war-dance. Two mighty warriors across the seas will send us arms.

"Tecumseh will soon return to his country. My prophets shall tarry with you. They will stand between you and the bullets of your enemies. When the white men approach you the yawning earth shall swallow them up. Soon shall you see my arm of fire stretched athwart the sky. I will stamp my foot at Tippecanoe, and the very earth shall shake."

The mass of followers remained still and silent during his speech, but as Tecumseh was nearing the end, the setting sun was transforming the sky into brilliant shades orange and red. When he shouted the line about "fire stretched across the sky," he threw his arms into the air and pointed upward, and when the crowd witnessed the red sky, they jumped to their feet with an earsplitting roar of cheers and shouts, as if they believed the great Tecumseh had just changed the color of the sky.

Most of the braves in attendance agreed with Tecumseh's words. They knew they needed to do something drastic to stop the masses of white settlers from invading, and they were grateful to have a strong leader, especially someone with the fierce reputation that followed this mighty warrior.

Not everyone on the field agreed with Tecumseh's words, however. An aged warrior stood in the back of the throng, listening closely to Tecumseh and eyeing the responses of the raucous crowd. His wrinkles creased his face even more deeply as he frowned at the group's enthusiastic reaction. His dark eyes narrowed at his Creek brothers, who seemed to blindly accept the words of the warrior. In his many decades as the Great Chief of his village, he had seen this kind of fervor before, but he wasn't convinced warfare was the answer to their difficulties. The young warriors in front of him did not have the experience he had. They did not know the devastation a full-blown war would create. The old man stood with his arms folded across his chest and did not applaud. He waited to hear more from Tecumseh, but after a few minutes of roars that didn't seem to be dying down anytime soon, he rolled his eyes, turned, and slowly walked away, leaning on his cane for support. His spokesman, Hillis Hiya, followed him, and together they ambled silently across the large field until they reached the Great Chief's animal-hide tent near the edge of the woods.

"Mekko, do you want to return home now?" Hillis Hiya asked.

"No, I want to speak with Tecumseh. Please get word to him that I'd like to meet with him as soon as possible. Tell him I will be here until sunrise, at which time he has lost my support if he does not come."

Hillis Hiya nodded and bowed as he backed up a few steps. He then turned and walked back toward the still cheering crowd, heading directly to the platform where Tecumseh was speaking only moments ago.

Later that evening, Tecumseh arrived at the Great Chief's tent in the company of a small crowd of supporters, carrying torches to light the way.

Hillis Hiya greeted him. "Good evening, Tecumseh. Thank you for coming."

Hillis Hiya gestured with an open palm for Tecumseh to enter the tent, and Tecumseh motioned for his followers to remain outside.

Hillis Hiya gestured toward the small braided rug in the middle of the floor. "Please be seated, and I will inform Mekko you are here."

Tecumseh sat down on the rug and placed his elbows on his knees. He looked around the tent, thinking it very nice lodgings. Mekko certainly knew how to travel in comfort. There was a bedroll and an assortment of bowls and cups neatly stacked in the corner. A glowing lantern filled the tent with warm light.

Hillis Hiya returned moments later, carrying a tray that held a long-stemmed pipe, some dry tobacco, and a jar. He carefully placed the tray in the middle of the rug.

"Beer," informed Hillis Hiya when he noticed Tecumseh eyeing the jar.

Hillis Hiya crumpled the dry tobacco and had just finished filling the pipe when the Great Chief entered the tent. He quickly rose and disappeared through the flapping door, leaving the two great men to speak alone.

"Tecumseh!" The Great Chief held out his hand in greeting and smiled as he entered the tent.

"Mekko, it's good to see you." He shook the Great

Chief's wrinkled, bony hand. "Hillis Hiya said you wished to speak with me. I hope you are anxious to join the cause."

The Great Chief slowly lowered himself onto the rug across from Tecumseh and gestured for the warrior to be seated. The chief adjusted his long coat and placed his cane on the rug next to him. He then took a sip of beer, and handed the jar to Tecumseh. Tecumseh drank, then set the jar down on the tray. The chief then proceeded to light the tobacco pipe. He took a long draw from it and handed it to Tecumseh.

After the chief exhaled, he finally spoke. "Tecumseh, you certainly have a motivational way of speaking."

The warrior smiled and drew from the pipe. The sweet smell of tobacco filled the tent.

The chief continued. "The cause you speak of is exactly why I wanted to meet with you. If you don't mind clarifying, I didn't understand a few things you promised in your speech."

"I'll be happy to explain, Mekko. What do you wish to know?" Tecumseh exhaled smoke from the tobacco and watched it wafting upward. He handed the pipe back to the chief.

"First of all, how do you plan to protect my warriors from American weapons?"

Tecumseh paused. "I don't really know the answer to that. My prophets said no Creeks would be injured or killed in the battle, and I have to believe them. They have never led me wrong, as they are always truthful."

The Great Chief frowned, but he continued with his next question. "All right. My second question is, when will the British arrive with arms and ammunition for us?"

Tecumseh narrowed his eyes. "Why do you question me?"

"I want to make sure my braves will not be injured and that they will have the necessary weapons to fight this war. Are these not logical questions?"

"I told you the British will supply arms."

"But you did not tell me when."

"Why isn't my word good enough for you?" The volume of Tecumseh's voice was increasing. "I was but a child when I witnessed my father brutally murdered by a white frontiersman. My family moved from village to village and saw each destroyed at the hands of the white men during and after the revolution. Following the revolution, I formed a band of warriors who attempted to block the expansion of the white man into the Ohio Valley. The effort was successful for a time, but in the end saw no lasting result, for the white man kept coming—coming in droves. Conflict with the white man is a battle I've fought my whole life, and now in my forties, I know the stakes are high. We have to put an end to these Americans once and for all. The coming battle will be the resolution of all we pray for. If we don't fight, I fear it will be the end of our kind."

"I know your history, and I appreciate your determination, Tecumseh, but you must realize I've fought this battle twice as long as you have." He paused to allow the warrior to recognize his age and experience. "Before I commit to your cause, I would like a little more proof than a crowd of enthusiasts and speech full of empty promises."

"They are not empty promises, Mekko. I am a

mighty warrior. My reputation speaks for itself."

"Yes, it does, but I still want proof."

"You want proof?" Tecumseh hastily rose to his feet. "I'll give you proof. At daybreak, I am returning north for a battle at Fort Detroit. When I am victorious in that encounter, I will stomp my foot on the ground and it will shake your entire village." He pointed his finger at the Great Chief. "*That* will be your proof."

Tecumseh stomped out of the tent, leaving the Great Chief alone to smoke his pipe.

War is Coming

"So, what are you saying, James? You want to pack all of our belongings, our animals, and our children, leave Tennessee, and move to some wild Indian territory that's not yet settled?"

He sipped his coffee and nodded. "Yes, that's exactly what I want to do."

"What about the children? What about their school?"

"We'll do what we have to do, Elly. We'll school them ourselves if that's what it takes. This is a great opportunity, and the timing couldn't be better. The government is selling that land for next to nothing, and we'll have twice the property we have here. Our farm will be twice as large, earning twice the money. And honestly, with what's going on in the North, I don't think we should stay here any longer. It looks as if we're going to declare war upon the British. They're already fighting up there, and I'm afraid the fighting is going to move its way down here. I would rather school the children myself than to take a chance on them living in the middle of a conflict, or worse, dying in it."

She looked at him in disbelief and didn't know

what to say. He had a tendency to exaggerate, so she didn't know if he was being truthful or purposefully saying shocking things about the children's welfare to get her to agree to move.

He continued. "During the revolution, my father was too old to fight, but he housed many soldiers who related vile tales of death and destruction. He told me stories of the horrors. Men who weren't killed or injured in battle often starved and died anyway. Women and children were often caught in the crossfire. I don't want to sit here and watch history repeat itself. The revolution gave us our independence, but the British are still dominating and oppressing us. We still don't have the freedom we desire. That's what they're fighting for in the north— freedom. I agree with what they're doing, but I don't want my wife and children caught in the middle. I think there's going to be a second revolution. After what my father told me about the first one, I can't help but be fearful that this one is destined to be the same."

"Yes, I know the stories. I've heard them myself. But I don't know about moving, James." She shook her head as she lifted her skirt to stand. She walked away from the table and placed her coffee cup on the counter. "I don't know how to pack all of our things and start all over. It seems impossible."

He sipped his coffee again and grimaced. It had grown cold. He placed the cup down on the table and looked at her. "I don't think we have a choice, Elly. The war is coming. We have a good opportunity right in front of us to avoid the whole situation, to start fresh, and to keep the children safe."

She leaned her back against the counter and placed

her hands on her hips. "What about Indians? Aren't there Indians there?"

"Yes, there are, but I'm sure they won't be any problem. Other people live amongst them. And besides, we'll be buying the land from the government, not from the Indians. It will be our land, fair and square. At least we won't find ourselves caught in the crossfire because the Indians don't have guns. From what I've heard, they live off the land and keep to themselves."

She sighed, knowing he would not let this go. He wanted an answer right now, but she couldn't give him the one he wanted. She looked across the room and stared out the wavy glass of the window for a few minutes, trying to decide what to say. After a while, she folded her arms and looked at her husband. "All right, I'll make you a deal. You go and look at the land, and if it's nice and there are no Indians, I'll agree to move there." Her gaze returned to the window. "I'll miss Tennessee, though. We've both grown up here, our family is here, and our children don't know any other life."

He rose from the table and moved toward her. "We don't have family here anymore, Elly. Since our mothers passed away, we're pretty much alone here. Look at it this way. We are young and healthy, we don't have aging parents to take care of, and the children are all young enough that they have to come with us. They're not running off and getting married just yet. If we're going to go, now is the perfect time."

She nodded, knowing he was right. They were as free to move as they were going to get.

"And as far as your deal goes, I'll take you up on that offer. I'll leave first thing in the morning and be back in a few weeks. The boys can run the farm while I'm gone." He placed his hands on her hips. "Will you be all right here without me?"

She wrapped her arms around his neck and looked into his eyes. "How long will you be gone?"

"Probably a month. Six weeks at the most."

"Sure, I'll be fine. I'll miss you, though. I don't think we've ever been apart for that length of time before."

"No, I'm sure we haven't, and I'm going to miss you terribly." He kissed her tenderly on the lips. "But I'll be home before you know it, and then we'll pack and move onto our new land. You know, I hear it's flat and fertile terrain with no rocks." He grinned.

She smiled back at him. "Well, I'm excited about *that*. I can't count the number of ankles I've wrapped up because of tripping on those darned rocks."

"Beautiful land, no war, and no rocks. It'll be great, Elly. You'll see."

"I hope so."

He kissed her again and she melted into his embrace. After twenty years of marriage, he still had the power to make the entire world disappear.

Jack began to whimper from the other room, breaking their connection. Elly released her grasp on her husband, gave him a peck on the lips, and left him standing by the counter. She went into the bedroom, picked up the crying infant from his crib, and snuggled him.

"Good morning, little Jack. Daddy wants us to move to a place called the Mississippi Territory. Doesn't that sound like fun?" She bounced him in her arms and glanced out the window at her handsome husband, who was sauntering across the yard with a shovel over his shoulder. Jack whined. "Little Jack, do you want to move to a new place?"

His small cry became a wail.

"Me, either."

Hasse Ola

The humidity of the warm December night hung like a wet blanket as Tafv Hokkolen led the thirteen-year-old boy through the darkening woods. They walked without words between them as far as the night would allow. He and the boy looked alike, red skinned, high cheekbones, prominent noses, and jet-black hair shaved on the sides but left long on the top. They both wore tan buckskin pants, tattered suede moccasins, and no shirts. Their kind didn't wear shirts unless it was cold, and tonight was definitely not cold. Tafv wore a cow tail tied around his right bicep. The boy wore the same in an attempt to look more masculine. The only differences between the two were their ages and muscle mass. Tafv was in his early thirties and had the chiseled physique of a heroic, colossal warrior. The boy had many years ahead of him before he would reach that status. The elder always wore two hawk feathers sticking up on the back of his head, tied into his headband. The boy wore a simple porcupine headpiece.

Tafv stopped in the forest clearing and motioned

for the boy to sit down on a log that had long ago been a mighty poplar. When the boy took a seat, Tafv silently walked around behind him. He drew a piece of tan woven cloth from his waistband, removed the boy's headpiece, and tied the cloth around the boy's eyes. Tafv then removed a single brown-and-white hawk feather from the two he always wore and placed it on the back of the boy's head, tucking it into the knot of the blindfold.

A man of few words, he spoke soft and low. "When you feel the morning sun on your face, you may remove the blindfold and return home." He placed his hand on the boy's shoulder for an instant, and just as quickly, he removed it.

The boy didn't say anything. In truth, he didn't know what to say. He couldn't ask questions. He didn't want to appear afraid. He wanted to be brave in front of Tafv, but he felt his stomach beginning to quiver. He grasped the log beneath him in an effort to absorb its strength, as he was now beginning to realize how difficult it would be to remain here alone in the forest until morning. *You don't have to do anything but sit. Stop thinking like a child,* he chastised himself.

He listened for Tafv's footsteps in departure, but heard nothing. Tafv always moved in total silence, so the lack of footfall did not surprise the boy. He sat motionless and listened, waiting for the sounds of the forest to return. His bare arms and chest became cool as he felt the dampness of the woodland moisture beginning to rest on his skin, and he listened to the growing breeze rustle the leaves high above his head. He forced himself to relax his grasp on the log, and he slowly rubbed his thumb across its bark, caressing the roughness beneath him. It was quiet; he could hear his own breathing. He focused on that, wondering how many times he would have to breathe in and out before the sun rose. He thought he should concentrate on something tangible to keep his mind from wandering, or he might lose his determination. He could not allow his fear to grow and consume him. All warriors partook in this ritual. It was the way they became men. But it was immensely easier joking with his friends about spending the night alone in the forest than actually doing it. Being alone at night made him nervous. Being alone in the forest doubled his anxiety. Not being able to see anything was the pinnacle of the challenge, and he quickly felt his resolve cracking under the weight of his mounting fear. *Breathe in, breathe out. Don't be afraid. Breathe in, breathe out.*

As he sat motionless, the nocturnal sounds of the forest slowly permeated his consciousness. Crickets chirped in the brush and a katydid buzzed from high in a treetop. Soon, a chorus of tree frogs began to croak, and a snorting sound came from far to his right. The sound was familiar, and he identified it as a deer. The woodland creatures began to stir and scurry all around him. A clamor he didn't recognize came from his left. *Breathe in.* A strange noise sounded straight ahead. *Breathe out.* He knew the forest held dangers, but he chose to push thoughts of those out of his mind. Bobcats, rattlers, poisonous spiders, black bear, wild boar, even rabid opossum and raccoon lurked near. *Don't think about that!* He focused on his breathing.

Something scurried up a tree to his right. His heart rate quickened as he listened intently to the sound. He did not turn his head toward the noise. He remained still. *Breathe in, breathe out.* He listened as it climbed to the top of the tree, and he heard the rustle of leaves as it jumped to an adjacent tree in front of him, then another toward the left. After a few moments, it was gone.

An insect walked across his hand. He remained still and allowed it to go on its way. *Breathe in, breathe out.* He felt a bug bite his shoulder. He acknowledged the sensation, but did not move. The breeze increased in intensity and rushed loudly through the trees, chilling the dampness on his bare arms. He felt goose bumps on his flesh. Faint thunder rumbled in the distance. Would he be caught in a rainstorm? He certainly hoped not, but with the humidity in the air, he wouldn't be surprised. Maybe the sound was caused by the heat rising from the valley many miles away.

Something touched his ankle above his moccasin. He listened closely and faintly heard it move across the ground. A snake. A cottonmouth or rattler would strike him if he moved, so he remained motionless. *Breathe in, breathe out.* He felt the full weight of the creature's body as it rubbed across the top of his foot. It moved for a long time, and he wondered exactly how long it was. He could tell by its weight it was big. Abruptly, it stopped. He felt the slight sensation of its darting tongue repeatedly flicking across his ankle. *Don't move. Breathe in, breathe out.* After what seemed like hours, it slithered away.

He stayed still and listened to the sounds around him. Time passed, but he didn't know if it was moving quickly or slowly. He could have been sitting there for a few minutes or a few hours. He realized his hearing was becoming more acute. He heard an owl screech in the distance. *It must be miles away.* He visualized the movements around him. He felt he was becoming one with the forest. Every sound was now recognizable. Every fiber of his body was alert, yet strangely calm. *Is this what it's like to be a man?* Why else would his father demand this of him? Why would he be left out here alone to fend blindly for himself? The more he thought about it, and the more he melded with his surroundings, the more it made sense to him. He realized he did not feel the fear he initially felt. Instead, he felt an inner peace, a greater understanding, a stronger sense of himself. He was in complete control of his mind, his responses, and his reactions. He relaxed, and the tension released from his shoulders and forehead. His jaw went slack. He breathed deeply.

He heard a low grunt behind him. The hairs on the back of his neck stood up, and he felt the heat of adrenaline course through his veins. He listened for another sound from the creature, but could only hear the sound of his own racing heart pounding in his ears. He didn't move. He focused all his attention in the direction of the creature. Since there was no second grunt from the animal, he knew it wasn't a wild boar. That left only two possibilities—a black bear or a bobcat. Either could be deadly. He heard it slowly approach him, and visualized its velvet paws flattening the damp pine needles on the forest floor. It was directly behind him now. He could hear it breathing. The sounds that previously filled the night air had vanished. The crickets and tree frogs became hushed. Whatever was behind him had alarmed the entire forest into silence. The animal's breathing grew into a low, menacing growl, followed by a high-pitched shriek like a child screaming. A bobcat. *Remain still. Breathe in, breathe out.* He felt the creature's whiskers tickle the back of his arm as it sniffed his back. Then, as quickly as it had appeared, it grunted and darted off through the trees. He listened to it run away. Fast.

Why did it run off so suddenly?

A crow squawked above his head and he heard the flutter of wings. *Birds don't sing at night. It couldn't possibly be morning already.* Small animals began to scurry around him in a peculiar frenzy. He assumed the sounds were squirrels and chipmunks, but he couldn't be sure. *Shouldn't they be asleep?* The trees grew lively with a chorus of songbirds—crows, doves, sparrows. He knew their calls. *Why were they singing?* Since his arms still felt cool and damp, he knew the sun was not yet rising.

He felt his weight shift, but he didn't move on his own. He nearly tumbled off the log as his body pitched from one side to the other. A large tree cracked to his right, and made a thunderous sound as it crashed to the ground. He jumped at the sound but remained seated on the log. The rocking intensified, as did the animal noises. He knew something was happening, but had no idea what it was. He tried to remain still, but it was useless. It was as if the whole forest was moving. He was confused and startled though not frightened. He didn't even have to remind himself to breathe.

After a few minutes, the swaying stopped, but the daytime animals continued to scamper and shriek in protest to whatever had just happened. He could feel sweat dripping from his forehead, dampening the blindfold. His heart pounded in his ears and perspiration dripped down his back. He focused again on his breath, but his thoughts kept returning to what had made the earth tremble. Would it happen again? After a while, the animals quieted down but answers did not come. Neither did movement. The forest remained still. Was the experience his imagination? *No, it couldn't have been.* The animals would not have experienced it with him. Something had happened.

Thunder once again sounded, and he heard the light patter of raindrops on the treetops, but fortunately the drops were few and never broke through the canopy. After a few minutes, the shower stopped. He remained on the log, with a sense of uneasiness.

Hours later, the cool dampness of the night began to transform into a warming mist. He heard the first songbirds of the morning, bees began buzzing, birds sang in the treetops, and woodpeckers started their incessant knocking high above his head. He couldn't see the light through the blindfold, but when he felt the warmth of the sun on his face, he took a deep breath and sighed, half out of relief that the ritual was over, and half out of pride that he had conquered the unknown. He lifted his hands to remove the blindfold, finding his elbows and wrists stiff. He pushed the cloth up onto his forehead and squinted into the leaves above him. It was the greenest green he had ever seen. He looked around as his eyes adjusted to the light filtering sideways through the trees. The brown of the tree bark was the richest brown, and the smallest grains of dirt beneath his feet had a deeper texture than he remembered. Everything was more vivid. *Is this how a man views the world?* Was he indeed a man now?

He rose, laced his fingers together, and raised his arms above his head, stretching the tension from his back. *Now, which way is home?* He turned to look around and get his bearings, and was startled to see his father sitting cross-legged about fifty yards away, staring at him. *Has he been there all night?*

"Father, why are you here?"

Tafv rose to his feet and slowly walked toward the boy. "Son, you need to become a man in your own way and in your own time, but I will always be your father, and I will always watch over you."

The Earthquake

In the middle of the night, the log house began to rock back and forth. The intensity grew quickly, rolling James off the bed and depositing him rudely on the floor. Elly heard him moan, and at the same time, one of the children whimpered from the other side of the room. She bolted upright in bed, looked around the dimness, and swayed.

"James! What's happening?" she cried, realizing the whole house was moving.

"I don't know. Earthquake?" He jumped to his feet and grabbed his trousers from the post at the foot of the bed. He stepped into his pants as he ran to look out the window to see if someone was causing the commotion, an attack of some sort, perhaps. He held the linen curtain open with one hand and buttoned his trousers with the other. A small rectangle of light from the moon cascaded into the room and moved to and fro across the floor, in rhythm with the rocking of the house.

Elly glanced around the room. Their four youngest children were sleeping in their beds on the other side of the small room. The baby, one-year-old Jack, whined in his sleep. The others remained silent.

"Do you see anything?" Elly whispered, attempting to keep the tremble of fear from her voice.

James let the curtain fall closed, leaving the room in darkness. "No, not a thing."

Elly watched the shadow of the curtain sway side to side.

"I'll go outside and have a look."

Jack's whimper became a cry. James went to the child, staggering like a drunken man trying to navigate a cobblestone street. He picked up the babe and handed him to Elly as she rose from the bed. She took Jack in her arms and followed James out the door into the hallway.

When Elly passed the girls' room, she glanced in the open door and saw her daughter Sarah, sitting up in bed.

"What's going on?" Sarah asked in a hoarse whisper.

"I don't know, Sarah. Stay there," Elly commanded as she followed James toward the parlor, watched him grab his rifle from above the mantel, and march out the front door.

She lit the lantern on the table and looked up at the ceiling as small bits of debris dropped like a spring rain shower. The roof groaned in its shifting. Pots and pans hanging from hooks near the fireplace clanged softly against the stone hearth. She moved toward the door to await her husband's return, bouncing Jack in her arms to soothe him.

Then, just as suddenly as it had started, the shaking stopped.

Elly froze near the door, waiting for something else to happen. She watched the window's curtains become still. The clanging near the fireplace stopped. Her heart pounded in her ears as she wondered if the motion would begin again. Nothing happened. She heard something behind her and spun around. It was three-year-old Bo padding down the hall toward her, rubbing his sleepy eyes with his fists. She held out her hand to him. He shuffled to her and grabbed her nightgown, wrapping his arms around her leg and burying his face in her thigh. She rubbed his head. Jack had placed his thumb in his mouth and was falling back to sleep in her arms. She kissed his head as she patted Bo's shoulder.

Everything was now silent except for the animals outside. Through the open doorway, she could clearly hear the cows lowing in the field and the two hound dogs howling in the yard.

"Momma?" Sarah quietly called from the other room.

"It's all right, Sarah. Go back to sleep and we'll talk about it in the morning."

James ran back to the house and hopped up on the porch, out of breath, his face ashen.

"What was that?" she whispered. She closed the door after he came back into the house.

"It must have been an earthquake." He shrugged and shook his head. "I've heard of them, but I've never felt one before. Is everyone all right?"

"Yes, I think so." She looked down and stroked Bo's hair.

"There are some snapped trees and the roof on the chicken coop collapsed. We probably lost all our birds, but I'll have to wait until the sun comes up to go out and get a better look." He placed his gun back on the hooks above the mantel.

"Oh, no. Our chickens are dead?"

"I'm sure they were in their roosts when the roof collapsed, so yes, they probably are."

"Did you see either of my little goats? I don't hear them."

James wrapped his arm around his wife's shoulder. "No, I didn't see either of them. I wish I had better answers for you, Elly."

"As long as everyone is all right, I guess that's all we can ask for." She nuzzled into his chest.

They tucked the little ones back into their beds and checked on the other children. After the adrenaline wore off a little, James and Elly crawled into their own bed. While they put the little ones back to bed, Elly had lit the lantern on her bedside table, and she was leery to blow it out. They lay silently, staring at the ceiling for a long time.

She finally whispered, "A lot of debris fell from the ceiling. It's going to be a long day cleaning that up tomorrow."

"You and the girls can do that while the boys and I figure out what to do about the coop and clear those fallen trees. I hope that was the only damage. It was hard to see out there in the darkness."

After a few moments, Elly spoke again. "James, do you think that was God's way of telling us to go?"

He turned toward her. "I don't know that God would shake the whole earth to send us a private message, but I guess it's possible."

She turned toward him, admiring his chiseled chin in the dim light created by the small lantern. He smiled a reassuring smile. She smiled back, suddenly feeling guilty that she had been postponing the move he wanted to make. Uprooting her entire family from their home and friends in Tennessee didn't feel right to her, but he had been adamant that they would have a better life in the Mississippi Territory. He had already gone all the way down there to look at it. He had already purchased it. He was waiting for her to agree to move. Maybe God was telling her to stop being stubborn and go. She turned and looked up at the ceiling again and felt him do the same. They lay still, lost in their own thoughts. James reached for her hand under the covers and squeezed it gently,

Tafv and the Great Chief

In the first light of day, Tafv and Hasse Ola emerged from the woods on their return to their village. They walked down the empty main road, shuffling their moccasins on the dirt. Nearly one hundred mud huts lined either side of the street in neat rows. Except for a few dogs and chickens that crossed their path, there was no one milling around this early. The roosters were just beginning their morning song, and there was gray smoke just beginning to drift upwards from a few chimneys. Tafv smelled the sweet scent of wood burning and the aroma of flat bread and venison wafting from houses as they neared the village square. He loved this time of day when the world was quiet and beginning to stir, but this morning, he was tired. They walked all the way through the village toward their house on the other side, ready to retire after their long night in the forest. They were greeted by Eto Lecv, Tafv's brother.

"Good morning, brother," Eto said quietly. He eyed young Hasse Ola and smiled.

"Good morning, Eto." Tafv did not break stride, and his brother fell in beside him.

Hasse Ola nodded at his uncle and smiled back, slowing down and giving his uncle room to walk next to his father.

"Mekko wants to see you right away," Eto whispered, to not disturb anyone in the village with his chatter at this early time of day.

"I'm sure he does. The earth shaking last night probably has him greatly concerned."

"So, it wasn't my imagination," added Hasse Ola, picking up his pace to hear more about the earth shaking.

"No, son, it wasn't."

Tafv stopped and turned around to face Hasse Ola. "You go on home and get some rest."

The boy stopped and removed the single feather his father had placed in the back of the blindfold he was still wearing as a headband. He gently held it in his open palm, offering it back to his father.

Tafv took the feather and smiled, then placed it back in his headband with his other one.

"Good night, or maybe good day, father and uncle." Hasse Ola nodded to the men and ran off down the dusty road. Both men watched him as far as they could see him, until he turned left off the path and was gone.

"How did he do?" asked Eto.

"He did fine."

Tafv was filled with both pride that the boy was now a man, and trepidation that the aggression of the white man and division of the Creek people would soon lead to war. His son would now have to join the battle. This was a worrisome time, not only for him, but for all of his people.

The Creek clans were divided. Some villages sided

with the white man and had been learning the white man's ways, including farming and language, for years. Some were even marrying white women, bringing the white man's ways directly into the villages.

Other Creek villages were adamantly against the white man's ways. The white man had hunted their land to near extinction and decimated their herds of deer. Their sacred woodlands had been cut down. Their tribal lands had been turned to mud. These villages had fought the white man's encroachment for a hundred years. They refused to trade with the white man, and they would certainly not learn to read and write in the white man's tongue. They were not shy about running off the invaders or even killing them in cold blood if necessary. Scalping a white man was a symbol of honor and courage. It showed the strength and pride of the warrior who performed the act. The white man did not belong on Creek land. This is the way it had always been, as far back as Tafv could remember. Even his grandfather scalped the white man. His son would do the same.

With war now brewing between his people, the Creeks were in a battle for their way of life—not only against the white man, but also their Indian brethren who supported the white man. All of the recent skirmishes were bloody and deadly, and though Tafv's village elders had not made a commitment either way in the conflict, there seemed to be no resolution to the turmoil.

The worst part of the chaos was that every Creek was family. Each Creek was part of a clan, and the clans were brothers and sisters, so the Creeks who married whites were the ones caught in the middle of the dispute. They were the ones who brought the whites directly into the clans and asked their brothers and sisters to accept them. Tafv had friends who married whites, which broke his heart and angered him deeply. The whites had essentially invaded the Creek nation through marriage and caused brother to fight against brother. How were the Creeks supposed to preserve and protect their way of life, when their way of life was being eroded from the inside out?

Tafv solidly belonged in the group that believed the white man's ways would eventually destroy the Creek way of life. And once that way was gone, it would never return. He would rather perish in war than become one of those he despised the most.

When Tafv and Eto reached the village square, he thanked Eto for the message and walked alone toward Mekko's house. The Great Chief's home didn't look any different than the other homes in the village, but it was located in the center of the village, in the place of honor. All other homes were built out in rows, in accordance to where the chief's home sat.

Like all Creek homes, it was built of sturdy river cane and covered in mud plaster. The roof was thickly thatched and replaced regularly, keeping the home dry year round, even in the rainy season. As Tafv approached the modest home, he noticed smoke coming from the chimney and smelled the delicious aroma of stewing rabbit. His stomach growled. He noticed Hillis Hiya sitting on a rickety chair on the front porch, carving something out of a piece of wood. Hillis Hiya was the village's medicine man and public spokesman for Mekko, for the Great Chief never spoke in public. Hillis Hiya narrowed his eyes at Tafv as he neared the porch.

"Good morning, Hillis Hiya." Tafv nodded to the

medicine man.

"Good morning, Tafv. How did your son do in the ritual last night?"

"Very well, thank you. Eto said Mekko summoned me." He was tired and in no mood for idle chitchat.

"Yes, he did. Please go right in." Hillis Hiya watched the warrior rap lightly on the door before entering, not waiting for anyone to open it.

Inside, the hut was cool and dark. The walls were covered with warmly colored woven cloths, and the rug in the center of the floor was the skin of a black bear. Tafv felt he could lie down right there on the rug and sleep, and he hoped this meeting wouldn't take too long. He looked around the main room. It held only a small sofa covered in deer skin, and wooden table surrounded by six cane chairs, but on that table sat a feast fit for the Great Chief. The smell was intoxicating, and Tafv's stomach growled again. Freshly fried flatbread, stewed rabbit, and something with the scent of rosemary.

The chief's granddaughter, Talisa, was stretched over the table, lighting two lamps. When they caught their flame, they flooded the room with a soft, warm glow. Tafv stood silently inside the doorway, watching her and awaiting her invitation to enter the room.

Talisa was a beautiful twenty-five-year-old maiden who adored her grandfather and catered to his every need. She was tall and thin, and her cocoa-colored skin, darker than most Creeks', was warm against the bright pink mantle she wore. Her black hair lay in a braid down her back. She was lovely, and Tafv had a hard time taking his eyes off her. He knew that Talisa, being the granddaughter of the Great Chief, had many opportunities to marry, but she always turned them down. He'd heard rumors that she had feelings only for him, but he ignored those rumors. He had only one love—his wife, Nila. Sadly, Nila died shortly after she gave birth to Hasse Ola thirteen years earlier. It didn't matter if people circulated rumors, or how striking Talisa was, he still loved Nila with every ounce of his being, and refused to consider a relationship with any other woman.

He was not blind, though. He noticed all the maidens of the village would stop whatever they were doing every time he passed by them. They paused their digging in the gardens when he rode by on his horse. They stopped hanging their clothes on the line when he cut through the houses on his way to the woods. They giggled and whispered when he strolled through the square, and he knew they were speaking of him. He could feel their stares and their desire. He ignored all of them. He had spent the last thirteen years raising his son in the manner he had promised Nila he would do, and nothing else mattered to him.

When Talisa finished lighting the lamps on the table, she turned and spoke quietly to him in a voice of silk. "Tafv, please sit down and I will get my grandfather." She gestured toward the table with her open palm and smiled sweetly.

He tried to avoid her hypnotic gaze as he nodded and took a seat on the long side of the rectangular table.

He sat alone in the room and stared at the feast in front of him. He didn't know whether he was more hungry or more tired.

The Great Chief interrupted his thoughts when he appeared from behind an ornately weaved curtain that separated the rooms. Talisa held the chief's elbow, helping him toward the table. He allowed her to assist him as he walked, leaning on a cane, favoring one leg over the other. In the shadows of the lamplight, his intense eyes and deep facial lines were even more pronounced than usual. He was at one time a great and fearless warrior. Even in this decrepit state, he was a large, formidable man who commanded attention and respect. The chief slowly lowered himself into the seat at the head of the table. He ran his fingers through his white hair and looked at Tafv for a long moment.

"I'm glad you're here, Tafv," he said as he reached across the table for some stewed rabbit.

Tafv rose to bow to the Great Chief, but the elderly man quickly waved his hand for Tafv to sit back down. Tafv returned to his seat and glanced up at Talisa, who was standing behind her grandfather's chair, watching Tafv. She looked down at the floor when their eyes met. Tafv looked back at the chief, who was observing the interaction between the two.

"Please enjoy this meal with me." The chief gestured toward the food on the table.

Talisa set a brown plate made of pottery in front of Tafv.

"Thank you, Mekko. I am honored."

Talisa disappeared out the back door and reentered, placing more dishes of food in front of them. She set plates of more flatbread and bowls of cabbage and wild blackberries on the table.

"Tell me, how did Hasse Ola do last night?" The chief grabbed a handful of the berries.

"He did very well." Tafv spooned some cabbage and stewed rabbit onto his plate.

"Even through the earth shaking?" The chief raised his eyebrows and popped a blackberry in his mouth. Tafv was sure he saw a smirk on the man's lips, but he didn't understand the significance of it.

"Yes, sir. I think I was more stunned than he was by the shaking. It did not startle him in the least. He is now a brave, and he apparently has much more courage than I, for I was quite distressed by the shaking." Tafv smiled weakly, feeling Talisa watching him again from where she stood on the other side of the table.

The chief tore a piece of bread and placed it on his plate. "I'm glad he did well."

Talisa filled their cups with juice. The men ate in silence for a few minutes.

After a while, the chief spoke. "The earthquake is the reason I wanted to speak with you."

Tafv waited for him to elaborate. The chief took his time. He thoroughly chewed his bread and took a long, slow drink from his cup, eyeing Tafv the whole time.

Finally, he continued. "Did you speak with Tecumseh when he was here recruiting warriors to help fight the Americans?"

"Yes, I did."

"What did he tell you?"

"He didn't say much except that his prophet offered a prediction of a victory for the Creek people. The prophet said no Creek warrior would be injured or killed in a battle, and the British would supply us with weapons and ammunition. I don't believe we would not lose men in a battle of that scale. I don't care what his prophet said. And how will we know when or if the British will show up with support?"

Tafv shook his head. "Our people are too divided now. Following a war of that magnitude, I don't think we could ever go back to our way of life—even if we were victorious."

"That's exactly what I told him. I told him I require more proof than his prophet."

"How could he give you proof of that? What was his response?"

"I don't know if you want to hear this." The Great Chief stared intently at him.

"Just say it, Mekko."

The chief looked down at the table, took a deep breath, and sighed before continuing. "Tecumseh said he would head north and take Fort Detroit, and after his victory, he would stomp his foot on the ground, causing every house in our village to shake. This would be the sign that his prophet was telling the truth."

Tafv stared at the chief, his jaw open.

The chief looked back at the table and dunked his bread in brown juice from the stewed rabbit. "That is exactly what he told me." He nodded and shoved the bread into his mouth.

Tafv realized he was sitting there with his mouth agape, but the prediction was too unbelievable. He continued to stare at the Great Chief.

When the chief finished his piece of bread, he said, "Tafv, I believe he took Detroit last night."

Tafv said, "I'm speechless." He slowly shook his head in disbelief.

"I know this isn't the news you want to hear, but I believe it's time. It's time to go to war and defeat the white man once and for all."

"Mekko, you know this will mean killing our own.

There are too many villages that have taken up the white man's cause, and too many of our people who have wed them. This could destroy all of us, our entire nation."

"No one said it would be easy, Tafv, but it's time."

James and Elly

"Are you sure you're ready to do this?" Elly asked as she stood by the dining table that was covered in clean clothes and folded the baby's gown.

"Why? Are you having second thoughts again?" James replied, cocking his head.

"No, not second thoughts." She pushed a strand of hair from her face, then demurely looked up at him. She saw a sad expression on his handsome face, and it broke her heart. She knew he was discouraged by her bringing this up yet again, so she tried to reassure him. "My home is wherever you are. You know that. I just don't know how I'm going to pack an entire house and eleven children and travel halfway across the country."

"Elly, it's not halfway. It's only five hundred miles."

"It might as well be the whole country. We're leaving our friends and family. We're leaving our home, James. How are we going to rebuild this?" She waved one hand around the room.

He approached her. "This,"—he waved his hands around, too—"is only a house, much of it damaged

47

by the earthquake. We will build a new house, a bigger one. I built this one all by myself. Now I have two teenage boys to help me. Imagine how nice our new home will be with Hays and Absolom helping build it. And wait until you see the land, Elly. It's beautiful." His face lit up with a gorgeous smile, and his eyes twinkled with excitement. "There's a creek on the property and we won't have to move any rocks. There isn't one rock there at all. Planting will be so much easier without rocks." He gently placed his hands on her shoulders. "It'll be our own little slice of heaven. You're going to love it there."

She placed the baby's gown on the table and gave James her full attention. She was happy to see him so excited, and the thought of no rocks was very pleasant. They had spent over twenty years moving rocks, repairing plows, and healing animals lamed by the constant boulders. Every time they thought they had a field cleared, more rocks would be unearthed. It was as if they were dropping from the sky.

"I know it will be wonderful. I'm just feeling nervous about getting there."

"You always feel this way about anything that concerns the children. You'll feel better in a few weeks when we're on the trail." He kissed her forehead in his usual comforting way.

"I hope so." She lifted herself up on her tiptoes and kissed him on the lips.

He enveloped her in his arms and passionately kissed her. She welcomed the connection and entwined her arms around his neck. There was nothing on Earth she loved more than him. If he was happy about the move, then she knew she should at least put on a good front. When he finished kissing her, she smiled at him.

"It'll be great, Elly." He backed up from her embrace. "Besides, Lizzie is almost twenty now. If we don't go now, she's going to find a husband and start having children, and I know you won't want to leave once you have grandbabies to play with. We need to go now, while we can still drag her along with us."

"You're right. I guess it's now or never."

"The Mississippi Territory is the new frontier, and the piece of land we bought is perfect for us. It's perfect for farming and raising cattle and raising children. And do you know what else?"

"What?"

"As more settlers arrive, they'll need a blacksmith. I'll have more work than I'll be able to handle. We are going to make a lot of money, Elly."

She turned back to the table and picked up a pair of trousers to fold. "I'm sure it will be great, James." She placed the folded trousers on the edge of the table and paused for a moment before she broached the subject that was really bothering her. She didn't take her eyes off the table. "What about the Creeks?"

"I already told you I didn't see any Indians when I went down there. Even if they're close, I'm sure they won't be a problem. The government has been helping them for years, training them to be good American citizens. They've been schooled in reading and writing, and they've learned to trade. I think they'll probably welcome us when they find out I have the ability to make them anything they want."

She pulled her eyes from the table and looked up at him. "Are you sure about this?"

"Yes, I'm sure." He smiled and winked at her.

"Don't flirt with me, James. I'm thinking of the

safety of your children. I don't want to endanger them."

"There's no danger. I promise."

He leaned forward and kissed her forehead again, then bolted out the front door, leaving it wide open. She walked to the door and watched him walk toward the barn. He had a spring in his step she never remembered seeing before. She was happy to see him so excited. She just wished she felt the same way.

Powwow and Intruders

As the moon began its ascent into the nighttime sky, men placed large logs on the bonfire in the large field just outside the village. The flames reached their red fingers upward, lighting the entire meadow. Women began arriving from all over the village to the sound of rattles. Under their long skirts, they had gourds and turtle shells filled with river rocks tied to their legs, and the rattling sounded with each step they took. Children ran around the growing fire, laughing and playing. It was quite a festive atmosphere. It was not every day one of their own became a man. The whole village had no doubt that Hasse Ola, the only son of the great warrior Tafv Hokkolen, would become a valiant warrior like his father. This gala was in his honor, and it would be a great festival indeed.

As Tafv stood off to the side watching the preparations, Eto approached him and whispered, "Tafv, I need to speak with you in private."

Tafv nodded and followed Eto to the outside of the large gathering, along the far row of trees.

When they were out of earshot of everyone else, Eto said, "After you and Hasse Ola left last night, our scouts spotted a wagon of white men about five miles north of our village. We rode out there and confronted them. We took their rifles and told them to turn back. We also warned them to not hunt on our land."

"And?"

"The white men did not heed our warnings."

"Where are they now?"

"We found them again this morning. They moved about three miles closer to our village and set up camp. They also killed a deer early this morning."

"How did they kill a deer with no rifle? The white man is incapable of using a bow."

Eto shrugged. "We must have missed one."

Tafv looked off into the dark woods, his brow furrowed. "Why didn't you kill them last night?"

"We would have, but they had a young boy with them about Hasse Ola's age, so we thought for the safety of the child, they would do what we told them to do."

Tafv glanced toward the fire and the crowd gathering for the celebration. He watched Talisa approach the fire with her grandfather and Hillis Hiya. She moved like a deer herself, graceful and sure-footed. "What do you suggest we do now?" asked Tafv, already knowing the answer.

"We have to kill them now."

"Agreed."

"We'll leave at sunrise to take care of it."

"All right."

Tafv, finished with the conversation, took a step toward the fire, but Eto grabbed his arm. "Tafv."

Tafv stopped and looked back at his brother.

"Now that Hasse Ola is a brave, he needs to come

with us."

"Yes, I'm aware of that," Tafv snapped and yanked his arm out of Eto's grasp.

Eto looked at his brother with concern. "There's one more thing."

"What now?"

"I spoke with Mekko, and we want Hasse Ola to start the prayers tonight. We want him to celebrate his accomplishment."

Tafv nodded. It was a great honor for a man to lead the opening prayer, especially a young brave the age of Hasse Ola. Tafv knew Hasse Ola would be pleased.

Eto continued, "Then we want you to lead the second prayer and pray for Hasse Ola's safety. He is important to all of us, not just you. We don't want anything to happen to him."

Tafv gazed into Eto's eyes with no expression.

Eto didn't understand the look. "What is it, Tafv?"

"We need to pray for all of us, not just Hasse Ola."

Eto didn't respond. He waited for Tafv to elaborate.

"We're going to war, Eto."

"It's only a few white men."

"No, not them, not tomorrow, but soon. Tecumseh is the one who caused the earth to tremble last night. It was foretold to be a sign for the Indian tribes to ban together and fight off the Americans. And whether we experience victory or defeat in this battle, I'm afraid this will be the end of our way of life."

"Is that what you discussed with Mekko this morning?"

Tafv nodded. He watched Hillis Hiya step toward the fire to start the celebration. "Let's go back."

Tafv approached the gathering with Eto respectfully trailing behind. Tafv took his son by the arm and led him to the middle of the circle, where the Great Chief waited.

"Oh, Great Chief, leader of our people, I present to you our new brave warrior, son of Tafv Hokkolen and the late Nila—Hasse Ola."

Everyone applauded as Hasse Ola bowed before the chief.

Hillis Hiya stepped forward. "Hasse Ola, the Great Chief welcomes you to our band of courageous and fearless warriors and presents you with this." He handed Hasse Ola a turtle shell tied on a long stick. It was filled with river rocks and adorned with hanging beads, turkey and hawk feathers, and animal fur. "We would be honored if you would lead the first prayer."

Hasse Ola took the turtle shell from Hillis Hiya and bowed again to the chief. He turned to his father with a surprised expression. Tafv nodded to him, acknowledging the honor that had just been bestowed.

Hillis Hiya turned to the people, raised his arms, and bellowed, "Let the celebration begin!" Through the applause, the medicine man and the Great Chief backed up through the crowd and took their seats on the outside of the large circle. The men of the village stepped toward the fire, while the women and children stepped off to the side, giving the men room to dance. The crowd quieted, with all eyes on Hasse Ola.

Hasse Ola looked around the circle of people. He searched for his father and when he caught Tafv's eye, Tafv held his palm out toward the fire, gesturing for the young man to begin.

Hasse Ola approached the fire and began chanting as he shook the rattle and stomped clockwise around the large fire. Every sentence Hasse Ola uttered was followed by an echo from all the men as they joined in the circular dance. Tafv followed directly behind his son, beaming with pride, as the chanting roared among the trees and the flames lifted the prayer to the heavens.

The men made one pass around the circle, and when they returned to the starting point, the women fell into line behind them. With each stomp, the women's rattles increased the volume of the celebration. As more and more women joined in, the din grew even louder. Once the men and women had passed once around the circle, the guests began to join in, followed by the children at the rear of the line. Until tonight, Hasse Ola had always been in this last group.

The entire village celebrated all night long, with a series of rattling, chanting, and dances that Tafv was certain the white men, only a few miles away, could hear clearly. He hoped they interpreted it as a war dance instead of a celebration, and that they would pack up and depart immediately. He didn't have a problem killing the white man, but he was anxious about having his only son involved, especially scalping a young boy who was probably the same age.

Tafv looked around at his people and noticed Talisa watching him from the back of the line. She was stunning, wearing a turquoise mantle and a white ribbon tied around her neck. The brightness of the colors against her cocoa skin and long black hair was exquisite. She nodded and smiled at him. He gave her a weak smile in return. He then refocused his attention on his son and the celebration with no further thoughts of white men or the beautiful Talisa.

Engagement

Before the sun began its ascension into the morning sky, Tafv, Eto, Hasse Ola, and a handful of braves set out to the white man's camp. They crept through the woods and arrived at the settler's wagons before they had risen. They hid among the bushes and trees surrounding the campsite, and they waited.

"Eto," Tafv whispered, "how many did you say there were?"

"Three men and a boy," Eto whispered back.

"All right. I assume they're sleeping in the wagons. When we see them emerge, we'll kill the men, and we'll try to take the boy back with us."

"I'll tell our men to not kill the boy if possible." Eto rose from his crouching position and tiptoed around the camp to find the other braves.

The smell of magnolia and lilacs filled Tafv's nostrils and reminded him of his dear wife. She always smelled of flowers. The thought made him sad and disrupted his concentration. He looked over at Hasse Ola, who was not more than a dozen yards away from him, waiting in ambush. He was proud of his son, but sad that the boy would now see firsthand the brutality the Creeks used to keep their people safe and their land out of the white man's hands. He watched the boy. Hasse Ola was staring intently at the two wagons. His eager expression turned Tafv's stomach.

Eto returned to Tafv's side and reported that the braves now knew to keep the boy in the wagon safe if at all possible.

They sat quietly and waited. The camp was silent except for the crickets.

As the first ribbons of light appeared in the sky and the first songbirds of the morning could be heard, they overheard grumblings coming from one of the wagons and knew the men were rising. The first to emerge was a white-haired bearded man who looked to be in his sixties. Eto looked over at Tafv, who shook his head. Not yet. The white-haired man started a fire and placed a coffee pot on a rock in the middle of it.

A second man emerged from the same wagon, running his hands through his overgrown, bushy brown hair. He said something to the white-haired man and then walked to the other wagon to rouse its sleeping inhabitants. A discussion began between the man and the unseen occupants. Within moments, a young boy about Hasse Ola's age poked his head out of the wagon and smiled.

Tafv watched as the boy eagerly jumped out of the wagon and tucked his shirt into his trousers. He sat down on the dirt, wiped off the bottoms of his feet with his hands, and put on his socks and shoes. Tafv didn't know why the sight bothered him so much. Was it because Hasse Ola was witnessing the same scene? If Hasse Ola wasn't here, this scene probably wouldn't be as troubling to him.

When the final man emerged from the wagon, Eto looked to Tafv for instruction and Tafv nodded.

After a terrifying shriek from Eto, the braves followed with their own war whoop and the massacre began. The three men and the boy, startled by the noise, looked around wildly for its source. The braves emerged from the woods at the same time from every direction, surrounding the camp. The white men tried to get to their weapons in the wagons, but the Indians moved too quickly. The man with the white beard was hit on the head from behind with a tomahawk before he even took his first step. The bushy-haired man was cut down by Eto himself, collapsing in a ball where he stood. The third man tried to run from the camp, and Tafv gave chase. The man didn't get very far. After a few short yards, Tafv grabbed him from behind and slit his throat with a knife. After the man fell, Tafv grabbed his hair and sliced the bloody blade deep into the man's forehead, removing a large section of his scalp. Leaving the dead man in the woods where he fell, Tafv carried his trophy back to the camp.

When he arrived, Hasse Ola was standing next to the boy, whose body was in a heap on the ground. Hasse Ola held up the boy's scalp to show his father.

"Look, Father, I have my first battle prize!"

Blood dripped down Hasse Ola's arm as Tafv watched in horror.

"Oh, I see you have one, too." Hasse Ola smiled.

Tafv looked down at the scalp in his hand and back up at Hasse Ola.

Eto ran up to him. "I'm sorry, Tafv. Hasse Ola was on the other side of the clearing from the braves.

I didn't tell him you wanted to keep the boy alive."

Tafv didn't look at Eto. He continued staring at his son.

Hasse Ola, with an enormous smile on his face, asked, "Is that it? Are we to go home now?"

Eto left Tafv standing at the edge of the clearing and walked toward Hasse Ola. "Yes, that is it. Let's go."

They walked into the woods with Tafv trailing behind. At some point, Tafv dropped the scalp he was carrying, but didn't realize he had done it.

1812 on the Trail

Three months had passed since the first violent earthquake, and aftershocks were still felt frequently, frightening the entire Rodgers family and quickly convincing Elly they should make the move to the Mississippi Territory. Before the earthquakes, Elly wasn't enthusiastic about the move, but with each passing heave and roll of their land, she became more eager to head south.

Between the powerful aftershocks were two more massive quakes, one in January that collapsed the chimney, making it impossible to heat their home, and the other in February that destroyed their barn, killing two horses and one of Elly's favorite goats. With each quake, James and Elly packed their wagons faster.

As news of the earthquakes' devastation filtered in from around the countryside, they realized they'd have to be careful on their journey. Newspapers reported the quakes had caused rivers to overflow from their banks in various locations. Neighbors said bridges had collapsed and the quakes had caused massive crevasses to open up in the terrain. There were even terrible rumors of people missing, people who had apparently been swallowed by the earth.

Finally, after months of laboring, with all their belongings packed, and all eleven children, a host of rabbits, goats, and cows, and their newly purchased chickens in tow, James and Elly set out on their great adventure, leaving behind the devastation they once called home.

Elly looked back at their house as they prepared to pull away, and a tear rolled down her cheek.

James rode up to her wagon on his horse. "Are you all right?"

She smiled a wistful smile. "Yes, it's just sad to leave our home. There are so many memories here."

"I know, and we'll make new memories in our new home."

"You're right." She wiped the tear from her face and forced a smile. "We will."

He winked at her, adjusted his hat on his head, and snapped his reins.

"Let's go!" he yelled as he rode toward the front of the oxen-pulled wagon train.

Everyone coaxed the animals and they slowly plodded forward, leaving behind the only home the children had ever known. Elly tried not to cry for the first couple hours of their journey, without much success. Fortunately, she was in the back, so no one saw her.

There were three covered wagons in the caravan. Elly was in the rear wagon, filled with the seven youngest children, including little Jack, who tried to crawl out the back of the moving wagon at every opportunity. Behind Elly's wagon, tied to the back, were two cows. Lizzie, the eldest daughter, drove the second wagon, overflowing with rabbits and chickens stuffed into crates, piled in among boxes and baskets and various household items. Sixteen-year-old Sarah drove the front wagon that was loaded to the brim with furniture and farming tools. James and his two eldest sons, Hays and Absolom, rode ahead of the wagons on horseback to make sure the trails were clear and passable. They kept their eyes peeled for any signs of disturbance in the land, as the rumors of crevasses had James greatly concerned.

Though Elly was more inclined to make the move following the earthquakes, she was still very nervous about moving into Indian country. When the children were out of earshot, she told James she heard rumors that the Creek Indians were savages and scalped white men for no reason at all, but James assured her over and over again that the Indians were educated and civilized.

She replayed his words in her mind as her oxen marched forward on the rutted path. *There's no reason they would harm us or the children. We are not a threat to them. We'll trade with them and make friends with them. It'll be fine.*

"I sure hope you're right, James," she whispered to herself.

They wed when she was just a child of sixteen. She thought of Lizzie and Sarah and how young they were, but when she was that age, she was already married with children. In her two decades with James, he had always taken good care of her and the children, and she loved him more than life itself. She had always trusted his judgment and didn't see any reason to doubt it now. Besides, there wasn't much left of their home in Tennessee following the earthquakes. They had to rebuild, so it might as well be on the low-cost land the government was offering. They would have twice the land they owned before. There would be plenty of room to farm and raise cattle. Maybe when the children got married, they would build on the same land. It made her happy to think she could keep them around forever.

The days slowly passed, and the further down the trail they traveled, the more she accepted the fact it didn't really matter where they lived. James and the children were her life, so as long as everyone was together, it would be fine. By the end of the week, she felt better about the move. Once again, James had been right. Once they got out on the trail, she felt the weight of the damaged house, the fear of the unknown, and the stress from packing up all their belongings drain from her shoulders. As they sat around the campfire and ate venison and drank coffee, she realized she had not been this relaxed in months.

As the weeks on the trail dragged on into months, all of her fears vanished. She had a lot of time to think as she listened to the hypnotic clomping of the oxen, and she slowly convinced herself the Indians would eventually become their friends.

It took two long months for their wagon train to reach their new land, and when they were finally getting close, the land welcomed them with warm spring breezes and magnolia trees in bloom. When they took an afternoon break by a stream for the animals to rest, Elly sat on the bank and took off her bonnet, allowing the breeze to blow through her hair and the magnolia scent to fill her nostrils. The magnolia was her favorite flower, and she couldn't help but smile at the sight of the white blossoms. Her children splashed in the water and paid no attention to the beautiful surroundings. Everyone was weary and tired, especially the children. She noticed they were starting to bicker and get on each other's nerves. They had been patient and bored for long enough, so when they returned to the trail as the sun rose high in the sky, she allowed the middle-aged children to run alongside the wagons as long as they stayed to the sides of the trail and didn't get in the way of the oxen.

James trotted his horse back to Elly's wagon. "Are you sure it's all right for the children to play outside the wagon like that?"

"They've been cooped up for weeks. Let them run a little. It'll be good for them."

James didn't second-guess her. He brought his horse to a standstill and watched them running and laughing. He smiled.

Susannah, Polly, Harvey, and little Ellie were sprinting back and forth among the wildflowers. The girls stopped every few yards to pick flowers, then ran to catch up to the wagon and toss them inside to Peggy, who was making a huge bouquet. Bo and Jack slept next to Peggy in the rocking, creaking wagon, covered with tossed flowers. Harvey grew bored and began scouting for rocks. Occasionally, he would find a good one and throw it with all his might into the trees lining either side of the trail. Most of the rocks bounced off tree trunks before they went very far, but Harvey kept searching for more rocks to try again. Elly turned around to look on either side of the wagon often, keeping an eye on them and laughing at their silliness. James slowly rode next to the wagon, and she caught his eye. He winked at her. She smiled and thought her husband was the most handsome man she had ever laid eyes on, and this was turning out to be a lovely day. They were nearing their destination, and her family was happy and healthy.

Suddenly, they heard Hays yell from the front of the wagon train, "Stop! Everyone stop!"

Elly pulled back on the reins and yelled "Whoa!" to the oxen. She and James looked up to see what the problem was. James rode up and told Lizzie and Sarah to halt their wagons also, and slowly the wagon train came to a stop. James trotted forward as Elly instructed Peggy to get the children back in the wagon and keep them there. She jumped down from her driver's seat and ran toward her sons. They were atop their horses, staring at the ground on the right side of the trail.

"What is it?" James yelled to the boys as he neared.

"Indians, Pa," Hays answered.

Elly ran up to the men, her long skirt leaving a trail of dust in the air as it dragged along the dry ground. When she neared them, James commanded her to go back, but she ignored him and came face to face with the gruesome scene. She reached a hand up to her mouth and let out a small cry.

The sight before her made her heave. Six bodies were strewn about the ground next to the trail—four adults and two small children—all scalped. The next thing she saw was blood—brown, dried blood covering the grass and flowers and splattered on the surrounding trees. The clothing of the victims was covered in the dark color, as were their faces. Then she heard the buzzing. Flies were swarming around the decomposing corpses, hundreds of them. The scene was the most horrifying she had ever witnessed, especially the children who lay with their eyes open, staring blankly at the sky. The smell was worse. She pulled a handkerchief from her pocket to cover her mouth and nose.

"This happened recently, Pa. Maybe within the last day or so," Hays said.

Absolom looked into the trees to the left and the right.

James said, "They're long gone by now."

"But where did they come from?" asked Absolom. "There's no wagon."

"The Indians probably stole it," said Elly, as she stood next to her husband's horse and gazed at the horrific sight. "This is a warning." She looked up at James with eyes as big as saucers. "We're in Creek territory."

White Man

Hasse Ola bounded into the house, sweat beading on his forehead from the hot afternoon sun. He found his father sitting quietly at the table, carving an apple. The room was cool and dark, with only a small window providing light. He plopped down in the chair on the side of the table and without a word, his father handed him an apple slice.

"How are you today, Father?"

"Fine. Where have you been?"

"I was out hunting with the other braves." He bit the apple slice. "Why didn't you go with us this morning?" He wiped apple juice from his lip with the back of his hand.

"I didn't feel like it."

"Are you all right?"

"What do you mean?" Tafv focused his attention on the apple and did not look up.

Hasse Ola popped the last bite of apple into his mouth, wondering if he really wanted to broach this subject with his father. He wasn't sure what kind of reaction he would get, but knew he needed to bring it up sooner or later. He looked down at the table as he spoke to appear nonconfrontational.

"Father, may I speak freely?"

"Of course, son, what is it?"

"I've noticed you becoming more and more solemn the past few months and I wonder if something is wrong."

Tafv handed Hasse Ola another slice, which Hasse Ola took without looking up. Tafv placed the knife and the apple core on the table. He looked at his son for a moment. "You know, you look just like her."

Hasse Ola looked up. "Like who?"

"Your mother."

"I didn't know that." Hasse Ola could have sworn he saw tears in his father's eyes, which was something he had never witnessed before. "You loved her very much, didn't you?"

"I don't think love is a strong enough word. She was my sun, my moon, my life. Still is, I guess." He reached for another apple from the bowl on the table.

"Is that what's bothering you? Do you miss her?"

Tafv cut into the apple before answering. He dug the knife into the skin with precision.

"It's not that I miss her more than I usually do. It's just...I made her a promise, a promise I don't think I can keep."

"What promise?"

Tafv sighed. "You don't know this, but I guess you're old enough to hear the truth. Your mother was working in the garden, the one on the edge of the village square by the woods. She had gone into labor with you while working in the field and was on her way home when a white man appeared out of nowhere and shot her in the back. She barely made it back to the house. She had to crawl. And she was

bleeding to death. We couldn't stop the bleeding. Your uncle Eto chased the man down and killed him. I wasn't there to protect her, and I'll never forgive myself for that." He looked down at the table and paused. "She was giving birth to you, but she was bleeding profusely from the wound. She knew she wasn't going to survive, and she was saddened that she wouldn't get to see you grow up—all because of the white man's hatred. She made me promise to raise you in Creek traditions and to honor our way of life for all time."

"I didn't know she died that way." Hasse Ola looked down at the table, too, trying to absorb all that his father had told him. Abruptly, he looked up. "But you've fulfilled your promise. I am a man now. You've raised me according to her wishes."

Tafv handed his son another apple slice. "Have you noticed how many white men have come to our land?"

Hasse Ola nodded. "It seems there are more and more with each passing day."

"There are. For many years, I thought we could stop them from coming. I thought we could kill them off and that would be the end of it. But they keep coming, and I no longer think it's possible to stop them. They are destroying our fields and hunting our animals. They are marrying our people." Tafv shook his head and place the apple down on the table.

"We can stop them. I am a warrior now. I can help."

"You are young, Hasse Ola. You are courageous and strong, but you do not know the history or understand how futile it is to keep fighting the same battle with the same outcome. In the long run, we are going to be the ones who are destroyed, maybe not our bodies or our villages, but certainly our way of life. It's already happening. So many of our people have already given up the Creek ways and learned to read and write in the white man's tongue and to use their tools. Our ways, our lives are disappearing."

"We still have a good life, Father. Why does this upset you so?"

"Mekko told me we are soon going to war against the white man. Thirteen years ago I promised your mother I would raise you to be a brave warrior, but now I have an increasing dread that the life of the Creek warrior will end in either shame or death."

Building a New Life

Elly watched from the shaded comfort of the front seat of the wagon as her husband and teenage sons raised the walls on their new home. They had made a pulley system out of hooks and ropes and were heaving and sweating as they raised first one log into place, then a higher one, then the next. She looked around at the property. Crepe myrtles and magnolias speckled the clearing, and a few hydrangea bushes would bloom any day. Tall, spindly pines lined all four edges of the clearing, and the family had already made a path to the creek on the north side of the property. It was only a short walk to the creek, so they would always have a fresh water supply and wouldn't have to dig a well or collect rain water as they did back in Tennessee. Although Elly loved the flowering bushes and trees, she thought the creek was the prettiest part of the land. It was about knee deep and four feet across, surrounded by azaleas and dogwoods, with the occasional wild blueberry and blackberry bushes interspersed in the underbrush. Yes, it would be a beautiful homestead once it was finished. When the house was completed, they would plant a garden and start building a barn, and this place would become their own little slice of heaven. James wasn't exaggerating. The land was flat and fertile. It was perfect for farming and raising cattle. And there were no rocks here! She smiled as she realized twisted ankles would be a thing of the past for her family. The only rocks here were the large boulders on the riverbank, perfect for sitting on while doing dishes and laundry but impossible to trip over. She liked those rocks. She liked every single thing about this property.

She fanned herself with a fan made from thin pieces of pine bark as she watched the men work. She felt a little guilty for resisting for so long the idea of moving. It was certainly beautiful here. Maybe the massacre they stumbled across on their journey was caused by a band of traveling Indians. She frequently found herself glancing over her shoulder, constantly looking for Indians, but since they hadn't seen a trace of a single one, maybe none lived around them.

Little Jack squealed and bounced on Elly's lap as she admired the strength of her husband's bare shoulders glistening with sweat in the hot afternoon sun.

"Jack, you will grow up to be a handsome and strong man like your daddy."

The child giggled as she held him under his arms and let him jump up and down on her legs. He wiggled and tried to free himself from her grasp so he could climb down from her lap, but she held firm.

"No, no, you stay here with Momma. You don't need to toddle over there and get in the way."

She watched Lizzie and Sarah walk into the woods carrying buckets, laughing at something as they strolled together. They were also helping with the house building. They hauled heavy buckets of water up from the creek as Peggy, Susannah, and Harvey mixed the water with clay and straw to make bricks, which would be used later for the fireplace and the cookhouse. Dozens of wooden molds were scattered across the yard, drying in the sun. It could take up to a couple weeks for the bricks to harden, but they would be invaluable in protecting the house from the flames in the fireplace.

Little Ellie, Polly, and Bo were all napping in the back of the wagon. Elly was anxious to get them into a real house with real beds, but they didn't seem to mind sleeping in the wagon. Real beds would be nice, but she was more concerned with being able to keep them in a single secure place, and the wagon wasn't it. She smiled at the thought of them soon lying in their beds in their own room, and she began to hum a lullaby for Jack, who had finally settled into her arms and was looking drowsy. She watched her boys work on the house and the young ones laying out bricks in the yard. For this small moment in time, everything was in order. The children were happy and healthy, the house was coming along, and the new land was everything James had promised.

Jack placed his thumb in his mouth and his eyelids grew heavy. She rocked him gently and hummed. He was falling asleep in her arms. She kissed him on the forehead, then looked up and watched Lizzie and Sarah again emerging from the woods with full buckets of water. Her beautiful girls were laughing and smiling, which filled her heart. As they reached the edge of the tree line, something directly behind them caught her eye.

The man sat motionless in the darkness of the woods, astride a huge black steed. His chest was bare, except for a few beads and feathers dangling from his necklace and his headband. His bare arms were muscular, with a thin band of something wrapped around his right bicep. His face was covered in red and black paint, but through the color, Elly thought she could make out his high cheekbones and square jaw. On top of his head were two feathers sticking straight up. They twisted softly in the gentle breeze. His face held no expression as he sat stone still and watched her family. His body was that of stone, and for a moment she thought he was a statue, but what kind of statue would instantly appear in the wilderness? He slowly turned his face toward her, and she realized in shock and horror exactly what she was looking at. When their eyes met, a shiver went up her spine.

"James!" she whispered, but he couldn't hear her over the sawing and hammering and the children's chatter. Without taking her eyes off the stranger, she cupped her free hand around the side of her mouth and said "James!" more loudly. The sawing and hammering continued.

Reluctantly, she looked away from the stranger and in the direction of her husband. "James!"

He still didn't turn toward her.

"James!" she finally yelled, shocking Jack from his sleep and making him cry.

James stopped sawing and spun around.

She pointed toward the woods where the Indian was silently watching...but he was gone.

War

"I don't know what we're going to do, Mekko. I have traveled to all the neighboring villages, and found that half of our people are joining Tecumseh and half are siding with the white man. No matter who ultimately wins this war, we have effectively split our nation in two. Forget the white man; we are at war with each other."

Mekko looked down at the table at his untouched plate of food, his elbows on the table and his fingers tented. "I was afraid this would be the outcome of Tecumseh's speech. What do you suggest we do, Tafv?"

Tafv focused on the Great Chief, trying unsuccessfully to ignore Talisa, who sat across the table. She stared at him with her big, brown eyes. "I'm not sure. We've kept the white man off our land until now, but it seems they're coming in droves. We need to unite to rid ourselves of them, but I hate to spread violence toward our own kind. I've never before seen our own people killing one another."

"Me, neither. It's a very sad time." Mekko shook his head and took a small bite of venison.

Talisa rose and walked around the table to refill Tafv's cup with a fruit drink. He nodded at her and took a sip. Her lips curved into a small smile.

"I don't have any clarity about this, Mekko. I've never known this confusion before."

"What do you think is clouding your judgment?"

Tafv stared at his plate for a moment. "I think the idea of Hasse Ola getting involved in this chaos is weighing heavily on my heart. You should have seen the excitement on his face when he scalped that young boy. I was stunned." Tafv picked up a bite of venison, then placed it back on the plate. "We have always been prideful in our battles, but the exhilaration on his face disturbed me greatly. We have always fought our enemy with respect and honor." He picked up the venison but placed it back down again. "You know, losing his mother was hard enough, but the thought of anything happening to him, especially in a battle that is going to destroy us anyway, is inconceivable. The whole situation is all so senseless."

"It is not senseless. You love your son and don't want to see anything happen to him. I can tell you as a father myself, that's completely understandable, but with or without our children and grandchildren,"—he glanced at Talisa—"in the picture, we still need to make a decision as to which side of this war we will commit to, the white man or our people."

"When you put it that way, there is no decision to be made. We must defend our people."

"Yes, I knew you'd come to that conclusion, Tafv."

"So, we must join Tecumseh."

"Yes." The Great Chief took a bite of venison and

frowned as he found it cold. He pushed his plate toward Talisa.

Tafv nudged his full plate toward her also. She picked up both plates and left the room.

"All that being said, Mekko, I have discovered new white people on our land. It's a large family with nearly a dozen children, and they're building a house a few miles west of here."

"Building on our land?" The lines across the chief's forehead became deeper as he frowned. He glared at Tafv with bloodshot eyes. "What are you going to do about this?"

"I think I have a new idea, if you'll hear me out."

Mekko nodded for him to continue.

"When we kill the white man, we leave no one to spread the word to others. I don't think they ever get the message that they are not wanted here. So, I've been thinking about this and came up with the idea that we should frighten them off our land instead of killing them. We will make it impossible for them to live here, but leave them alive to tell others to stay away."

"How will you do this?"

"We'll kill their animals, destroy their crops, and burn their buildings. Then they'll leave and spread the word that our land is inhospitable. It will take time for word to get out, but once it's out, hopefully they will stop coming."

"That makes sense, and you must follow your heart. But realize the white family you found cannot be allowed to stay." Mekko's voice was at the same time understanding and firm, giving Tafv the impression he just received permission to try his new plan, but with strict instruction to eradicate the white family immediately.

"I understand. We'll move quickly. The white family has already cut numerous trees in our forest, and they have almost finished building their house."

Mekko rose from the table as Talisa reentered. He slowly turned to leave, dismissing Tafv. Talisa moved quickly to help her grandfather. "You do what must be done, Tafv. Keep me informed," the chief said over his shoulder as he left the room.

"Yes, Mekko." Tafv rose from his chair and bowed as the elderly man disappeared behind the woven curtain.

Taunting

Elly woke to the first dim light of day. She rubbed the sleep out of her eyes and listened to the sounds of morning. The birds were beginning their daily chorus, and the chickens clucked outside as they pecked the ground for morsels. She felt chilled and damp from the long night. She hated being damp. She longed to move into their house with a real roof so she wouldn't wake each day with the morning dew on everything she owned. She listened for her family, but none of them was stirring. James was snoring softly next to her. She lifted her head and looked over at the little ones. It was rare to wake up to the sound of silence, and she treasured the moment. She decided to hurry down to the creek, bathe in peace, and put on some clean clothes before the children woke up. She crawled out the back of the wagon and slipped on her shoes. She knelt down next to a wooden trunk near the back of the wagon and raised the lid slowly, in an effort to keep it from creaking on the rusted hinges. She grabbed a clean dress from the trunk, closed the lid, and tiptoed across the yard toward the clothesline. She grabbed a towel from the line but found it still damp. She sighed; she'd have to use it anyway. When their house was finished, she would be able to hang towels inside by the fireplace and they would be dry in the morning. The thought made her smile.

She crept across the wet grass, and one of her pet goats bleated loudly as she passed.

"Shhh," she chastised the animal.

The animal bleated again.

When she neared the almost finished house, she stopped dead in her tracks. The four walls that had been put up yesterday were no longer standing. Only the frame was left. She stared in disbelief at the logs littering the ground. *How did this happen?* she thought. *They couldn't simply fall down on their own. And why didn't we hear this?*

A branch snapped in the woods in front of her. She looked past the frame of her house into the dark trees and saw the Indian with the two feathers sticking up from the back of his head. She watched as he jumped onto his horse with no effort at all. Then her eyes caught more movement in the woods. She scanned the area and saw more Indians, maybe a dozen or so. They quickly disappeared through the trees without a word or a sound.

She dropped her dress and towel on the grass and ran back to the wagon, past the again bleating goat. She jumped into the wagon and shook James.

"James, wake up!" Her voice was a hoarse whisper.

"What is it?" he mumbled.

"Indians! They destroyed our house!"

James was immediately awake. "What?" He jumped up, grabbed his rifle, and bolted out of the back of the wagon, wearing only his nightshirt.

"They're gone now." She followed him as he ran

toward what was left of their house.

"How did this happen?" His eyes darted between examining the house and scanning the woods.

"I saw them running away. It was the Indians. They destroyed our house."

She watched James stomp around the frame of their home, stepping over pieces of logs and bricks, his face full of disbelief and fury. He again scanned the woods. He looked back at the house and back at the woods, as if debating whether he should chase the Indians or begin rebuilding.

"James," she said softly.

He turned toward her, looking as if he just realized she was standing there.

"Are you sure we're safe here? They're obviously telling us to leave."

He stepped toward her and took her hand, a look of determination on his face now. "Elly, they're not going to run us out. This is our home." He squeezed her hand. "We won't be frightened away that easily. We'll rebuild the house—better than before."

He wrapped his arm around her shoulder and she snuggled into his chest. She could hear his heart pounding. He was angry, and once James was angry, he became adamant. She knew he wouldn't leave this place now. He had something to prove. She wanted to believe every word he said, but after seeing this destruction, she wasn't sure he was right.

Plan to Scare

The Great Chief had summoned Tafv for an update on the white family. Tafv entered his house and stood in the doorway, delivering his report. "We destroyed their home a few weeks ago, but they didn't leave. They are rebuilding...and planting."

"It doesn't sound as if your plan worked. Why don't you just kill them all?" Mekko hobbled toward the table, Talisa by his side.

"Killing the white man has never done any good. They're arriving in record numbers, and I sincerely believe we have to change our tactics and scare them out. It may take a little longer to accomplish than I initially thought."

"So, what are you going to try next?"

He emphasized the word *try*, and Tafv realized the Great Chief was not in a good mood this morning. The aged warrior sounded almost sarcastic, as if he'd known Tafv's plan wouldn't work but let him try it anyway so he could get the silly idea out of his system. When he failed, as he just had, the chief would then order the murders of the white family. Mekko was an accommodating and compassionate man; it was not like him to act this way. Tafv hoped he was reading something incorrectly in the chief's tone.

The elderly man fell into the chair with a moan and a look of pain, and Tafv realized maybe the tone of voice wasn't because of his mood but his health.

Talisa handed her grandfather a cup. As he shakily held it in both hands and slurped from it, she looked at Tafv with a worrisome expression. Tafv didn't know what was wrong or if he could do anything to help the old man. He would have to find a moment alone with Talisa to inquire after her grandfather's health. He didn't look forward to being alone with the maiden, and shook his head in frustration.

"We'll make it worse for them, Mekko. We'll invade their homestead again and kill their animals and destroy their crops. They'll surely give up and move on then."

"I hope you're right. It sounds like a logical plan, but we all know the white man is not a logical creature. If they are not gone soon, I will order their slaughter. For now, do what you must. If it makes you feel good to not kill them, then so be it."

"It's not about feeling good, Mekko." Tafv heard the frustration in his own voice and took a breath before he continued. "But the ways we've gone about getting rid of the white man in the past have never worked. It's time for a change. There's no point in killing them if it's useless to do so."

"Well, you are the great warrior of our village. I suggest you take your men over there tonight and get rid of them any way you can."

"Yes, Mekko." Tafv bowed and backed out the doorway.

Tafv walked through the village, directly to Eto's

house.

Eto lived on the edge of the village, his front door facing a large field to the west. It was the field the village held their powwows in, the field where all the ceremonies took place, but when it wasn't filled with every person from the village, Eto undoubtedly had the best view of any house in the entire village. Tafv knocked on the door and was quickly greeted by Eto.

"Good morning, Tafv. How are you on this beautiful morning?" Eto was smiling and energetic.

"Gather a couple braves for me to return to the white man's tonight," Tafv snapped.

"I'm fine. Thanks for asking."

Tafv ignored the remark and looked out into the field.

"What's wrong, Tafv? You seem angry."

"No, not angry, just frustrated." He shook his head and began to walk away. "At any rate, gather the men. We'll return to the white man's after dark and destroy his animals."

Tafv was confident killing their livestock would force the family to leave. With a family that large, a house destroyed, and no garden planted, they would go hungry without their animals. No man would allow his children to starve, not even the white man. Then again, Tafv had thought destroying their home would run them out, but that didn't work. He hoped this plan would see a better result.

At dark, Tafv, Eto, Hasse Ola, and two other braves set out with bows and arrows and tomahawks. They would run this white family off their tribal land, and they would do so tonight.

Confrontation

After Elly first spotted the Indian, James had reassured her over and over that the Indians would not bother them. He told her the Indian had probably just come to see who they were and what they were doing, and as soon as they found a way to communicate with him, they might even become friends. He had repeated himself so much, she wondered if he was trying to convince her or himself.

After the Indians destroyed their house, James ramped up his narrative to a whole new level. She was ready to leave immediately, but he put his foot down.

"Elly, it's just going to take a little more time to build."

She was out of patience. "James, I'm tired of this whole thing. Why don't we just go back to Tennessee?"

"Our house there was almost destroyed, too. It'll take time to build no matter where we go."

"But there are no Indians in Tennessee."

"Yes, but there are rocks, and a dozen years of poor harvests because of those rocks."

"But rocks don't carry bows and arrows."

"Elly, they didn't shoot at us. They're just trying to scare us off the land. We'll rebuild. I'll have you in your new house in a couple of weeks."

She stomped away toward the creek, with a basket of dirty clothes under her arm. He followed her. She didn't speak to him. They were at a stalemate. In the oppressive heat of the afternoon, she plopped down on a boulder on the riverbank and scrubbed dirty clothes as she listened to her husband start up his diatribe yet again.

"When they find out the Rodgers family has much more endurance than they could ever imagine, they will stop torturing us."

James stopped talking for a moment, bent down, and cupped his hand in the cool water to get a drink. He pulled out his handkerchief, dipped it in the water, and wiped the back of his neck. She was grateful for the momentary silence. She felt him watching her as she scrubbed his shirt against the rock with a large brush.

When she didn't respond, he started up again. "Elly, we're not leaving here. They will have to get used to us. We have determination and fortitude. Perhaps they'll even grow to respect us one day."

"That's crazy talk, James. The Indians don't care how much fortitude we have, and they don't even know what respect is. They want us gone—period. And I tend to agree with them. We should leave. If we can't go back to Tennessee, then we should find another place to live. They'll never accept us. Obviously, by what they did to our house, they won't even tolerate us."

"Oh, they'll tolerate us all right. They don't have any choice. In a few months, when the fall harvest comes in, we'll trade with them. They'll welcome us then. We'll be in a warm and cozy house. Where do they live? A tent?" He bent down, picked up a flat stone, and skipped it across the water. "And when they get a taste of your apple pie, they'll come here every day asking for more."

She rolled her eyes at him and let out a heavy breath. "I don't want them coming here every day for any reason. With the way they've ruined our property and the time it's going to take to fix it, we're not going to have a harvest. We'll spend the entire summer building and rebuilding instead of working our fields."

"We'll get it all done. The boys are working the house, and I got a large plot of the field turned over to plant corn and wheat. We'll get it all done."

She kept her eyes on her wash and didn't reply.

"Well, I've got to get back to work." He started to walk away, but then turned back. "Sooner or later, those Indians will become good neighbors. You'll see." He winked at her and turned toward the house.

Elly shook her head. She wanted so desperately to be a supportive wife, but it was becoming more and more difficult. Every day she longed to pack up and go back home. She still thought of Tennessee as home, but she knew moving back and admitting defeat was not something her husband was going to agree to, and the thought of two months traveling again with the children in the wagon didn't appeal to her, either. The idea almost brought tears to her eyes. She felt caught between a rock and a hard place. She didn't want to stay here; he didn't want to return to Tennessee. The only thing she was positive about was she didn't want to sleep in the wagon for one more night.

After a few long and tiring weeks of rebuilding their home and getting the fields ready to plant, the entire family was exhausted. The house was nearly finished and they would start to move their belongings into it the following morning.

They all climbed into the wagons at dusk and everyone fell right to sleep. As they had done since they arrived, Elly and James slept in the first wagon with the two youngest sons, Jack and Bo. The girls—Lizzie, Sarah, Peggy, Susannah, little Ellie, and Polly—slept in the second wagon. The three boys—Hays, Absolom, and Harvey—slept in the third. The family dozed off to the songs of the crickets and katydids, accompanied by the babbling creek that could faintly be heard through the dense pines.

Elly struggled to sleep—over-tired, her momma used to call it. She was filled with anticipation of moving into her new house in the morning and everything that must be done, and she knew she must get some sleep but she was too restless. Once she finally fell asleep, it was a fitful slumber. She heard someone calling her, but wasn't sure if she was dreaming or awake. At first she thought it was one of her children, but she listened closely and realized it was the bleating of one of her little goats. She opened her eyes. No, she wasn't dreaming. She was sure of it. She listened more intently, for it was strange the goats would make noise in the middle of the night. She listened for the sounds of a predator. Perhaps a bobcat or a bear had wandered onto their homestead. She heard nothing. Even the crickets that were so vocal just a short time ago had gone to sleep. She again closed her eyes. As she began to doze off, she heard a faint thud, like something small hitting something solid. Her eyes popped open, and she heard a second thud. *What is that noise?* One of the chickens cackled and abruptly went silent. The chickens never made noise at night. Something was out there, something that shouldn't be. She sat up, straining to hear if one of the children had gotten up, perhaps for a drink of water. She heard only silence.

A moment later, another thud. One of the horses neighed.

It wasn't something that was out there. It was *someone*.

"James, wake up! They're back!" Elly whispered as she shook his chest.

"What?" He sat straight up.

"The Indians. They're back." She kicked the blanket off her legs and crawled toward the curtain covering the opening in the back of the wagon. She pulled it back an inch. The bright sliver of the summer moon painted faint shadows on the ground. She didn't see anything unusual in the yard.

Thud.

Another chicken squawked and silenced.

"Arrows!" James declared.

"What?" she looked at him.

"Those are arrows! Get down and protect the children," he commanded in a whisper.

He motioned for her to move aside, then he loaded his musket and stuck the barrel out the back of the wagon. He pointed it into the nighttime sky and pulled the trigger.

Boom!

Jack and Bo both slept through the gunfire, but Hays and Absolom came running toward their parents' wagon.

"Get down!" James yelled when he saw them. "Indians!"

The boys hit the ground and crawled on their bellies the rest of the way toward their parents' wagon. James handed Hays a long rifle out the back of the wagon. Absolom already had his pistol in his hand. They all remained still and listened, their eyes scouring the tree line. Nothing moved. Then they saw them—Indians in the woods. Elly couldn't tell exactly how many, but there were at least two or three.

"Let's run these savages off once and for all," said James as he quickly put on his trousers and shoes. Without tucking in his shirt, he climbed out the wagon. The trio looked in all directions, but even with the help of the clear sky and the bright moon, they saw nothing.

Suddenly, three Indians on horseback emerged from the woods and galloped right past them, through the yard, past the almost finished house.

"Let's go!" James said to his boys, motioning toward the corral.

The three ran toward their horses, but only one horse was standing. The other two were lying on their sides with arrows sticking out of their ribs. James ripped open the corral gate and didn't take the time to see if they were still alive. He threw the reins around his horse's neck and jumped on its back. It scampered and pranced, nervous about the night's happenings.

"Stay here and guard the family," James told the boys.

Out of habit, Hays closed the corral gate after James rode through, then he crouched back down between the horses, eyeing the woods. Absolom checked his horse. He placed his hand in front of its nostrils to see if it was still breathing. He shook his head sadly.

Elly stuck her head out the back of the wagon, one shaking hand holding the curtain open and the other holding a loaded pistol. She watched her husband ride off into the darkness to confront the Indians—alone.

When her eyes fell upon a small furry mound in the middle of the yard, tears rolled down her cheeks. It was one of her little goats, lying on the ground, unmoving, with an arrow in its side.

Burial

Mekko and Eto observed Tafv from Eto's front porch. Tafv was sitting cross-legged on the ground in the far end of the field. He stared at the mound of dirt in front of him, unmoving. The strong, invincible warrior looked like a sad and tragic figure. He hadn't moved from that spot for three days. He hadn't eaten. He hadn't spoken a word to anyone. Even his two feathers were hanging forlornly down the side of his head.

"Please explain to me what happened," Mekko said to Eto.

"I'm not really sure, Mekko. Tafv, Hasse Ola, and I, and a couple other braves were firing arrows at the white man's animals, and we killed all of their chickens, cows, and goats, and some of their horses. We didn't bother with the oxen because Tafv said he wanted the white man to be able to pack their wagons and leave. Then the white man came out of his wagon and fired upon us with his gun and we fled. We didn't get one of the horses, so the white man chased us on horseback. The other braves took off the moment they heard the shot. We followed as soon as we mounted our horses. Tafv took the lead, I rode second, and Hasse Ola was right behind me. We rode the long way around the creek and thought we had lost the white man, but when we turned around to check, we realized Hasse Ola was not with us. We retraced our steps, searching for him, and when we got back to the creek, that's when we found his horse, but no Hasse Ola. We searched the creek on foot and as daylight came, we found his body on the bank a little distance upstream."

"Did the white man kill him?"

"I don't think so. He didn't have any wounds on him except a bruise on his head and it looked like his neck was broken. I think he fell from his horse crossing the creek, but Tafv said it doesn't matter how he died. He said even if the white man didn't touch the boy, his son is still dead because of the white man."

Mekko looked back at Tafv and slowly shook his head. "I witnessed a dark change in him after Nila died, but he focused his anger and pain into being a good father. Without Hasse Ola here to keep him grounded, there's no telling what he'll do now."

"It's worse than that." Eto frowned.

The Great Chief raised his eyebrows in a questioning manner.

"The only thing he has said in the last three days is that blood will be spilled for this, specifically the white man's blood. He has vowed revenge against the white man and his family."

The chief sighed. "Well, we wanted them gone anyway, but killing for revenge will not be good for Tafv. He won't be able to live with himself."

After a few moments, the chief continued. "I'd like

to speak with you both at my house. Will you please bring Tafv there as soon as possible?"

"Of course, Mekko. We'll be there shortly." Eto bowed as the chief turned and hobbled down the dusty road.

Eto didn't know how he was going to convince Tafv to leave Hasse Ola's grave, but he walked over to Tafv and quietly kneeled beside him.

"Tafv?"

Tafv grunted.

"I know you're in mourning, but Mekko asked me to bring you to his house. He said he wants to speak to us both. Please come with me. There's nothing else you can do here."

Tafv didn't look up, but he nodded. After a long moment, he rose and walked across the field toward the road. Eto, mesmerized by the grave, and lost in his own thought, did not rise and follow.

"Let's go," he murmured to Eto, not looking in his direction.

Eto quickly jumped up and trailed after his brother. When he caught up to Tafv, they walked in silence as Eto didn't know what to say. They had already argued about the cause of Hasse Ola's death. They had already discussed Tafv's need for vengeance. They had already mourned the loss of the young warrior. Eto couldn't think of any other words that would be necessary, and certainly none that would make either of them feel better.

When they arrived at the Great Chief's house, Talisa opened the door and ushered them in. She started to say something to Tafv, but Mekko emerged from the other room and interrupted their greeting. He told the men to be seated. Talisa bowed to her grandfather and left the room.

Eto sat down with the chief, but Tafv stood at the side of the table, silently drumming his fingers on the wood, lost in thought.

"Please sit, Tafv," said Mekko.

Tafv reluctantly pulled out a chair and sat down, folding his hands on the table. He stared at his fingernails that were still caked with dirt from burying his son. Eto glanced at the dirt on Tafv's hands and realized he should have told Tafv to wash before coming into the Great Chief's home, but it was too late now.

"Tafv, I am so very sorry for your loss."

Tafv nodded.

"I called you and Eto here because I have some news."

Tafv remained focused on his fingernails.

"Tafv, this is important. I need you to pay attention."

"I'm listening, Mekko." His gaze stayed on his hands.

Mekko sighed and looked at Eto then back at Tafv before continuing. "A few weeks ago, a party of Creeks traveled to Pensacola to obtain supplies for a coming battle. The Spanish governor promised to supply them with food, blankets, gunpowder, and bird shot."

Tafv looked up at the Great Chief.

The chief looked into Tafv's eyes and continued. "They picked up supplies a little at a time over a few weeks as to not draw attention, but someone down there figured out what was going on, and while the braves were bedding down for the night, some white men ambushed them."

Eto's and Tafv's eyes went wide at the news.

"Are they alive?" Eto asked.

The chief nodded. "Most of them. They scattered in defense, and the Americans confiscated all of the supplies, even their horses. Late into the night, our men went in for a counterattack and ran off the Americans."

"So, we didn't lose the supplies?" Eto asked.

"No, we didn't, but other elders have called for retaliation for the ambush and for the deaths of a few of our own." The chief looked at Tafv.

"We're at war, then," Tafv stated without emotion.

"Yes, we are. We are planning a major attack in reprisal for the violence heaved upon our Creek brothers. Eto told me you would like revenge on the white family for your son's death, but I have to ask you to hold off for a little while. I need you both to go south right away. There is a fort about thirty miles north of Mobile, and warriors from many of our villages are meeting just north of there to prepare for the battle. We are going to destroy the white man's fort and everyone in it."

Tafv, still expressionless, nodded. "We understand, Mekko. We'll leave at first light."

Tafv rose from the table and Eto followed his lead. Tafv started walking toward the door, stopped, and turned back around. "What's the name of this fort?"

"Fort Mims."

Fort Mims, August 1813

A few days later, Tafv and Eto arrived at the meeting place near Fort Mims, and were amazed by the number of warriors present. There were more than a dozen villages represented and warriors totaling nearly one thousand. Tafv shook his head in disbelief.

"What is it, Tafv?" whispered Eto.

"Look at all the warriors here. There can't be this many people living in a fort. The white man's forts aren't that big." His brow furrowed. "This isn't going to be retaliation. This is going to be a massacre."

One of the young scouts ran past Tafv and Eto on his way to the war council's tent. The brothers glanced at each other and nodded at the same time, thinking the same thing. They followed the scout to see if they could hear some news of the coming battle.

The scout, who wasn't any older than Hasse Ola, entered the large tent without introduction and was warmly received. Tafv and Eto followed him and remained just inside the doorway. Eight men were in the stifling hot tent, discussing war plans around a large table. Since all attention was on the scout, no one noticed the two men near the entrance. The scout was short of breath when he approached the table. One of the men handed him a cup and he gulped down its contents, dribbling a little down his bare chest. He wiped his chin with his palm and nodded a thank you to the man. When he finally caught his breath, he reported, "The fort's gate on the east side is blocked by drifting sand. They can't close it. It's wide open. They can be easily attacked from that direction."

"Anything else?" asked one of the leaders.

"We observed that they always eat at high sun, and they always bring their guards in at that time. They are completely vulnerable. If you charge the open gate at that time, you'll catch them all inside."

One of the elders smiled. "That's very good news. Did you get an estimate of how many people were in the fort?"

"It looked like four or five hundred, sir."

"Very well. We'll attack tomorrow at high sun," the elder said. He turned to one of the other men and ordered, "Tell everyone to be ready to go in the morning."

The scout nodded and left the meeting. Tafv and Eto watched silently from the doorway as the council began making plans.

Word spread through the warriors' camp like fire through dry tinder. The men began sharpening their arrows and knives, preparing their horses, and mixing flowers and berries to be used as war paint. The anticipation rose quickly and furiously.

When night fell, no one slept, especially Tafv.

***

At high sun the next day, the Creeks charged the

open gate, catching the fort's inhabitants off guard. Amid flying arrows, swinging clubs and tomahawks, and the cloud of dust rising from the scuffling of nearly one thousand Creeks and five hundred Americans, Tafv listened as women screamed and children cried. He didn't look around for the sources, but the voices struck a deep sadness within him. He pictured the faces of his dear Nila and his brave son. A deep pain churned inside him, but he knew he had to keep his focus. Instead of allowing himself to feel his own loss or even his growing remorse for his people's current actions, he concentrated on the task at hand—killing as many Americans as possible. Last night, he and his fellow warriors had been instructed by the counsel that everyone in the fort must die, without exception—men, women, and children.

The opening of the battle was mostly hand-to-hand combat, but since the warriors had caught the Americans unaware and unarmed, the Creeks' objective was accomplished swiftly. After the first few minutes of intense fighting, over one hundred people were lying on the ground in various awkward positions. Tafv had a moment to catch his breath, and he stopped and looked around the interior of the stockade. The ground was littered with fresh blood and the deceased. He thought about his many conversations with the Great Chief about killing the white man and wondered if killing this many Americans at once would do any good. Killing a few at a time had accomplished nothing.

After the first onslaught and the initial surprise attack was over, the Americans began to man their weapons. Many left the fighting and returned armed, swinging their knives and stabbing with their bayonets, and when the first round of musket fire rang out, the Indians fled in haste to the distant trees.

As Tafv ran to the tree line, behind him he heard the Americans cheering in victory and was sure the sight of Indians fleeing was promising to them. But what the Americans didn't know was this was all planned, and they would soon learn that the concept of retreating was not something the Creeks were fond of.

Yes, the warriors withdrew to the tree line, and this is where they would initiate their second round of attack. The Indians' fire-laden arrows began hitting the stockade wall one by one. The dry, wooden fencing began to burn, filling the sky with thick, black smoke. Some of the Americans ran with buckets of water and attempted to put out the flames, but there were too many fires and not enough buckets, and the numerous fires grew quickly, and some of the bucket-carrying men died by flaming arrow before even reaching the wall. Within a very short amount of time, the stockade walls began to crumble in the dense smoke. Some sections burned to the ground, while others simply collapsed due to the lack of structural support. As spaces opened in the fence, the warriors aimed their arrows at the buildings inside, and one by one, those buildings caught fire, too.

The whole battle lasted nearly four hours, and in the aftermath, Tafv walked through the bodies and rubble that was all that was left of the fort. He stepped over soldiers, women, and children as he inspected the devastation. Hundreds of corpses littered the ground inside what used to be a safe haven. More bodies lay outside the burned walls. The entire population of Fort Mims, numbering at least five hundred, had either been killed or captured. Tafv had no idea how many scalps had been taken, but he knew the number was in the hundreds. He had a dozen or so stuffed in his waistband.

As he viewed the carnage, he realized the warriors had also killed many Creek brothers and half Creeks who had been living in the fort as American supporters. His stomach turned at the murder of his own people. It made him ill that his brothers had been killed, but even more upsetting was that these brothers were traitors. The sight made him both furious and sad. He needed to leave the area before he released the contents of his stomach all over the bodies at his feet. On his way out, he stepped over a scalped young woman who was still clutching her dead child. *This can't be right*, he thought. Death was not the answer. This massacre would not stop the white man from entering his tribal land. If anything, this would only enrage the white man and make matters even worse. He grabbed the scalps from his waistband and dropped them on the ground as he left.

The following morning, he and Eto started the journey back to their village.

As they walked through the trees, Eto asked, "Did that end as badly as I think it did?"

Tafv stared at the ground in front of him as he took one purposeful step after another. "Yes, I think so."

"So many people died needlessly. Maybe revenge isn't the answer."

Tafv softly said, "Maybe it isn't." Tafv knew Eto was referring to the white family on their land, but he refused to have the discussion.

They walked for the rest of the day in silence, both exhausted from the battle and awed by the events. When they stopped for the night and bedded down under a small cropping of trees, Eto brought up the subject again. "That battle left a sour taste in my mouth. How about you?"

Tafv, flat on his back on his bedroll, stared up at the stars and answered, "It was appalling. It made us look like the savages they say we are."

"So, now that you've experienced vengeance firsthand, are you still going to go after our white family?"

"Yes."

There was not another word.

Tensions Rise

Elly slammed her coffee cup down on the counter. She was livid at the whole situation and with her naive husband. She was certain he didn't understand the gravity of the situation. "James, the children are hungry. We don't have enough food to get us through the winter and now with everyone leaving, there's no one to buy food from."

"Not everyone is leaving. Stop exaggerating." He emphasized the word *everyone*.

She spun around and placed her hands on her hips. "You're the one who always exaggerates. I'm being realistic. Since the massacre at Fort Mims, over half of our neighbors have moved. I don't blame them. If it were up to me, we'd be gone, too. Those savages massacred hundreds of women and children down there…in cold blood!"

"Elly, those are a different group of Indians than our Indians. We're not dealing with those."

"Then what are we dealing with? Nice Indians who want to trade with us and be our friends?"

"Elly, calm down. The Indians here are just trying to scare us off. If they wanted us dead, they would have already killed us."

Elly stomped her foot. "Well, Indians or no Indians, we've been going without for a month now. How are we supposed to feed the children with no eggs and no milk?" She turned to walk toward the back door. "At least they left you a horse so you can ride somewhere and buy food." She picked up the basket of laundry sitting on the floor, held it against one hip as she opened the door, and turned to say, "Your children are hungry, James. I suggest you do something about it." She stomped down the steps into the yard, allowing the door to slam on her way out.

She realized she needed to get away from him before she said something she would regret. She marched across the yard, carrying the heavy basket of laundry. Usually she struggled with the weight of the basket, but she was so furious with her husband, the heavy load seemed to weigh next to nothing.

"Momma? Do you need help with that?" asked Absolom, who was tossing a ball in the yard with Harvey.

"No, dear, I've got it. I'll be back in a little while." She walked quickly through the trees, needed to get away from everyone for a little while.

James and the boys had spent the entire summer building and rebuilding the house, leaving no time to plant enough food to get the family through the winter. And what little they did get planted had been destroyed by the marauding Indians. What would happen if they ran out of food this winter? They had already gone without eggs and milk for a month. She worried about the children. She worried about their health and their future.

She angrily plopped down on a rock and yanked dirty stockings from the basket. She dunked them in the water and began scrubbing them hard enough to put holes in them. She could feel her ears buzzing and her shortness of breath and realized she needed to calm down. She stopped scrubbing, closed her eyes, and took a deep breath through her nose, trying to slow her heart. She concentrated on releasing the tension in her shoulders and the knot in her stomach. She felt guilty for losing her temper with her husband, but frustration was taking over her life. Every day brought new problems—life-and-death problems. Her mounting anger was overriding her fear of the Indians and her love for her husband.

She opened her eyes when she heard him clear his throat behind her, and she turned to apologize for her harsh tone of voice. But when she saw the black eyes looking back at her that did not belong to James, she stopped and gasped. They belonged to an Indian, sitting tall on a brown and white painted horse. She hadn't heard him approach. She jumped to her feet, wondering where she could run.

The Indian was bare-chested, wearing only tan animal hide pants and moccasins. His hair was short, shaved on the sides and sticking up higher on top. Most of the Indians she had seen had this same haircut. His face was covered with lines of red and black paint, and he wore a headband tied around his head with strips of animal fur hanging on either side of his face. His headband was not adorned with any feathers. This was not the same Indian she had seen before.

He stared at her for a long time and did not move. She glanced across the swift creek to the left and right, but there was nowhere to run. She would never be able to outrun a horse. Her heart beat wildly as beads of sweat broke out on her brow. She remained frozen.

"I came to warn you," the Indian said in a monotone.

Elly was surprised by his English.

He sat motionless, waiting for her response.

She finally blurted out, "Warn me about what? That you want us to leave? We already got that warning." She could feel her temper escalating again. All of the tension she had felt the last few months, all of the worry for her children, all of the stress of building a new life, was about to explode in this Indian's face.

"Yes, I'm here to warn you that you need to leave, but not for the reason you are thinking." He looked down at the reins in his hands, as if trying to gather his thoughts and find the correct words. "My brother and I were the ones who killed your animals."

Elly threw a wet stocking on the ground. She hadn't realized she was still holding it, and it had dripped down her blue linen skirt, causing the front of her dress to become dark in color. "You? You did that? How am I supposed to feed my children?" she raised her voice, her temper becoming stronger than her fear.

"This is the least of your worries. When your husband chased us away, my brother's boy fell from his horse and snapped his neck." His eyes carried a tint of sadness. "The boy is dead."

Elly felt her heart soften for a young boy she didn't even know. Her anger began to subside, as if it were being washed away by the babbling creek beside her. "I'm...I'm very sorry to hear that," she stammered, wringing her wet hands together.

"You must understand, my brother is the great warrior of our village. He has vowed revenge on your husband and your family for the death of his son."

Elly's eyes widened as the Indian continued.

"He told our Great Chief your husband killed his son, and the Great Chief has given him permission to slaughter your family."

Elly was shocked by the revelation and quickly shook her head. "No. My...my husband would never kill a boy. He's never killed anyone, for any reason."

"Our great warrior does not know this."

"Please tell him. Tell him my husband didn't kill his son." She took a step forward as she begged.

The Indian shook his head and looked at her with compassion. "I cannot tell him anything. I can only warn you. You must leave now...before it's too late."

Elly placed her hand over her mouth as tears stung her eyes. Her body began to tremble, and she turned her face toward the creek so the Indian would not see her cry. After a moment, she composed herself, wiped her cheek with the back of her hand, and turned back toward the Indian, but he was gone. She looked left and right through the trees, but it seemed he had simply vanished as quickly as he had appeared.

She left the wet clothing strewn on the rocks and ran as fast as she could back to the house.

Fort Sinquefield, September 1813

Elly ran all the way back to the house, yelling for James as she went, but when she entered the clearing, she noticed the horses and wagon were gone. She ran up the steps and into the house calling his name.

She found Lizzie rocking Jack to sleep in the bedroom. "Lizzie, where's your father?"

"Is something wrong, Momma?"

"I need to speak with your father right now. Where is he?"

"He took Hays and Absolom to Fort Sinquefield to see if they could buy some chickens and a goat or a cow."

"Did he say when he would return?"

"He said they'd be back late tonight. Momma, what's wrong?"

Elly backed out of the doorway, shaking her head. "Nothing, I just need to speak with him, that's all."

She marched into the parlor, pulled the long gun off the mantel, and loaded it. She then parked herself on the front porch and waited for James and the boys to return.

As the sun began to set and a blanket of dusk had fallen over the land, Elly heard the wagon wheels grinding on the dry ground. She stood up and leaned the gun against the house. When James and the boys pulled up, she walked off the porch to meet them. They carried a wagon full of chickens, two goats, and a hog. They also had a distraught-looking and very thin young woman in the front seat of the wagon.

The girl was dark-haired, wearing a black dress and dark gray bonnet. She glanced at Elly under the rim of the bonnet, then lowered her head so that Elly could not see her face. Elly eyed the young woman for a moment, but did not concern herself with who the waif might be. She ran to James's side.

"James, I need to speak with you in private."

"Elly," James said, "this is Eleanor. Eleanor, this is my wife, Elly."

Elly nodded at the girl, and the girl nodded back before looking down again at her lap. The poor thing looked terrified. Elly stared as Absolom, in the seat next to the girl, reached over and patted the girl's hand resting on her lap, offering her reassurances that she would be fine. The movement surprised Elly. She had never seen her seventeen-year-old son take an interest in a young lady.

Elly focused her gaze back on James and placed her hands on her hips. "James."

"What is it, Elly?" James hopped down from the wagon and waited for her to speak.

"Please, I need to speak with you," she whispered. She grabbed his hand and pulled him across the yard.

James turned and pointed at the animals in the wagon with his free hand, indicating he wanted the boys to take care of the animals. Hays nodded at his father as Absolom helped Eleanor down from the wagon. Elly walked fast in front of James, leading him toward the woods.

"Elly, if this is about Eleanor, I can explain. Her family was slaughtered by the Indians and she has no place to go. We saw her on the side of the road and thought we should bring her home with us."

"No, it's not about Eleanor." She stopped and faced him. "It's about the Indians."

"What about them? What did they do now?"

Elly shook her head. "I spoke with an Indian."

"What do you mean, you spoke with one? Here? Did one come here? Did he speak English? He didn't hurt you, did he?"

Elly sighed, exasperated. "James! Please listen."

"I'm sorry. What happened?" His eyes were wide with anticipation.

"I was doing the wash at the creek when an Indian appeared on horseback. He said he came to warn us that we should leave."

James raised his voice and started to turn toward the house. "That's nonsense. We are *not* leaving."

Elly grabbed his arm and stopped him. "It's not that simple. He said they were the ones who killed our animals, the ones you chased."

She watched his face grow red with anger. "James, before you get mad, please listen to me. He said when you chased them, an Indian boy fell from his horse and died. Did you see that happen?"

James shook his head. "It was still dark. The sun wasn't up yet, so I didn't see much of anything. I chased them down the road, but they turned to head upstream and I lost them. That was it. I didn't know where to look for them, so I came back home."

"The father of that dead boy is the village warrior. He thinks you killed his son, and he's declared revenge against our family."

"That's ridiculous. I didn't kill anyone. We'll tell them I didn't kill the boy." James's forehead wrinkled, as if contemplating how anyone could've thought he killed a child.

"I tried to tell him that, but he said the warrior won't listen."

James shook his head and looked around. He shrugged his shoulders as he said, "I didn't kill anyone."

"I know that and you know that, but this warrior is going to come after us. We have to go."

James looked into her eyes, reached out, and grabbed the tops of her arms. "For the last time, Elly, we're not going anywhere."

James spoke in an adamant tone Elly had never heard him use. It frightened her a little that he was so determined to stay here in harm's way. She didn't know what to say to him. Had his pride really grown stronger than his desire to protect his family? She didn't know what to think anymore.

He continued. "This is our home now. If the Indian you spoke with could speak English, then we can communicate with them and explain to them that I didn't have anything to do with it."

"That's not going to work. He said the warrior won't believe us." She pulled away from his grasp. "What are you going to do? Go over there and reason with them? Go over there and let them kill you, in hopes that they may or may not speak English and that they may or may not believe you?"

"I'll straighten this out." He gently pulled her into

his arms and she reluctantly moved into his embrace.

"I'm frightened for our children."

"I am too, Elly. You know I won't let anything happen to them. It'll be all right." He reached up and stroked her hair.

After a long moment, James released her and looked down into her eyes. "I have something else to tell you."

She didn't respond, but held his gaze. She knew something else was bothering him by the serious tone of his voice.

"We went to Fort Sinquefield to purchase some chickens, but the fort is gone."

"What do you mean, the fort is gone? Like Fort Mims is gone?" She backed away from his embrace.

He nodded. "We stopped and spoke to a man up the road from the fort. He told me it started a couple weeks ago when two families staying at the fort got tired of living there and returned to their homes."

She waited for him to continue.

He looked off into the distance at the towering pines across the road. "Indians murdered both families."

Elly gasped. "Our Indians?"

"No, I don't think so. The murders were too brutal. These weren't the kinds that kill chickens. These were savages."

"So, what happened to the fort?"

"The man told me one of the family members escaped during the massacre and ran miles back to the fort to get help. The next morning, a group of men from the fort traveled to the homes and found everyone had been murdered. They carried the bodies back to the fort to bury them, and when they opened the gates of the fort to pull the wagons in, they were ambushed. The fort was destroyed and everyone who survived the attack is now packing and heading south, including the man I spoke with."

"So, we don't have any neighbors at all now?"

James shook his head. "I don't think so."

Elly looked at the wagon, then back at James. "So, where did you get the chickens?"

"They were still at the fort. I just took them."

"And what about her? Where did she come from?" Elly looked at the girl standing by the wagon with her son.

"She said she had been staying with her grandparents and they had been killed by Indians, too. She had walked for three days and was on her way to the fort to get help when we found her about a mile north of the fort."

"Oh, James, what are we going to do?" She wrapped her arms around his waist and fell into his embrace.

"I don't know, but we'll figure out something."

She allowed him to hold her for a long time. She looked past his arm at Absolom and Eleanor, who were standing near the wagon. Eleanor was leaning back against the side of the wagon, and Absolom stood in front of her, only inches away. It was obvious her son was infatuated with the pretty girl. And by the way the girl looked back at him, the feeling was probably mutual. Elly wondered if Eleanor's family had thought they'd be safe from the Indians, too.

New Battle Plan

Tafv and Eto sat on a waist-high stone wall that separated the village from the open field. It was right down the road from Eto's house and faced the west, just like his porch. The hot evening sun in the cloudless sky bathed them in a wave of heat. They watched butterflies flitter in the wildflowers and the occasional bird crossing the clearing, traveling from the trees on one side to those on the other. The men sat quietly and waited for the sun to complete its arc and disappear behind the tree line. The sunset would entice the deer to come out of the woods for their evening grazing. The braves were ready for them, with bow in hand.

"I'm beginning to worry about you, Tafv," Eto whispered.

"I'm fine," Tafv retorted.

"No, you're not fine." Eto looked at his brother. "I haven't seen you this sad since Nila died, and it's been months since Hasse Ola died."

"What do you expect of me? I lost my wife, and now I've lost my only son." Tafv spoke softly, staring at the tree line.

From the right, Talisa and another young maiden appeared on the other side of the wall, walking down the road toward the village. The girls were on their way home, carrying baskets of walnuts they had gathered in the woods. Talisa wore a simple deerskin wraparound skirt and white blouse. The other wore a bright yellow mantle, embroidered and beaded with a rainbow of colors. Both had their long black hair twisted up on their heads in a topknot.

When the girls noticed Eto and Tafv sitting on the wall, they whispered to each other and giggled. Talisa purposefully dropped something as they neared, and they stopped so she could pick it up. The girls lingered for a few moments, both watching Tafv the entire time, but he never looked over to acknowledge them, so they reluctantly continued on their way.

After the girls moved on, Eto said, "Tafv, I'm sorry for your loss, and I have suffered loss, too. My nephew is gone. I don't want to lose you, too."

Tafv's shoulders slumped and he looked down at the bow in his hand. "I don't know what to do. After almost fourteen years, I still miss my wife so much. To fill that emptiness, I put every ounce of energy into raising our son, and now that he's gone, I don't know what to do with myself."

Eto didn't say anything.

After a long moment of silence, Tafv looked back up at the tree line across the field and continued talking.

"I also worry that the white man's destruction of our culture is not going to stop. I can't seem to come up with any ideas or ways to resolve it. Our brothers are fighting each other. Our land is being eaten up by the white man. There's no way to turn it around." He hung his head. "And since Hasse Ola is gone, I really don't see the point of even trying to do anything about it."

"Tafv, we can't give up. You are the great warrior of our village. If you don't lead the fight against the white man, who will?"

Tafv shook his head. "I don't care anymore."

"What about the white family? What about the revenge you vowed?"

Tafv shrugged. "What good would it do? The massacre at Fort Mims didn't do any good. Some of the whites left, but more came in their place."

"It would be good for the morale of our village to be rid of them once and for all. We ran out the others from the fort at Sinquefield. We can run this family off, too. We need to finish the job." Eto paused. "You know there are more children here besides our Hasse Ola."

Tafv rubbed the wood grain of his bow with his thumb. "What are you saying?"

"I'm saying there are more young men here who need a role model, who need training to become warriors, who need a safe village without the white man invading the nearby land. I'm saying you need to emerge from this sadness and go back to being the great warrior you have always been."

Tafv didn't move or respond. He looked across the field at a family of deer emerging from the woods. Four of them entered the field, and ever so slowly, Tafv reached over his shoulder and removed an arrow from the quiver on his back. He placed the arrow in his bow and rose from his seat on the stone wall. Eto armed his own bow, and together they tiptoed toward their unsuspecting prey. The deer looked around and froze every few moments, but always went back to their grazing. Tafv and Eto timed their movements with the grazing, and they froze when the deer froze. Soon, they were within killing distance, and both released their arrows at the same time. Two of the deer fell simultaneously, arrows in their hearts. The other two jumped back into the woods.

The men put their bows over their shoulders and continued walking toward their prey. Eto continued their previous conversation. "I've been over to spy on the white family a few times in the last months, and they've finished building a barn now. They have cattle grazing and crops planted. They are cutting down our woodlands, polluting our water and our land."

Tafv stopped and turned to his brother. He raised his voice in frustration. "What do you want me to do?"

"We need to run them out once and for all...or kill them."

Tafv looked down at the dry grass.

"We need you to lead us, Tafv."

Tafv sighed. "Do you have a plan?"

Eto smiled. "I do. One of the white man's older sons, the one they call Absolom, is to be married to a white woman in four days' time. I overheard them planning some sort of powwow in their barn for that evening."

A small grin formed on Tafv's face. "And?"

"And I suggest we set fire to the barn and everyone in it."

Tafv's eyes lit up.

Absolom and Eleanor

Elly stood back and admired the table decorations she had created. She had placed jars of purple and yellow flowers and tin lanterns on each of the three cloth-covered tables. The barn was filled with the rich scent of wild flowers, mixed with the delicious smell of the hog her husband was roasting outside. On each table, she set pewter plates and cups at each place. She was satisfied that the wedding celebration would be her best party yet. They would feast and celebrate and dance under the stars.

James entered the barn and looked around. "This looks really nice."

"Thank you. That hog smells wonderful, too." She moved a plate a little to the left.

"Elly, I need to tell you something before everyone comes."

She stopped what she was doing and turned toward him. Usually when he started a conversation with "I need to tell you something," it wasn't good news. She waited for him to continue.

"Absolom asked me for a wagon."

"What does he want a wagon for?"

James sighed. "After what happened to Eleanor, her grandparents getting killed and all, and now the attack at Fort Sinquefield, she wants to move out of Creek territory."

"Move? How far away?" Elly placed her hands on her hips.

She always knew her children would grow up and move away someday, and Lord knows, she wanted to move away from here also, but the knowledge didn't make the reality any easier to bear. The thought of losing one of her children had always weighed heavily on her heart, and now it looked as if it would soon become a reality.

"I don't know if they've decided on a location yet, but I knew you'd be upset about it, so I told him I wouldn't give him a wagon, but I'd help him build one. That will delay their move for a little while."

"I don't think they should move. I want them to stay with us." She stopped abruptly as she realized she sounded like her husband. She looked around the barn and sighed. "But, it's inevitable that our children will grow up and leave us, so I guess it doesn't really matter where they go or how soon they depart. It's going to be hard no matter what."

***

That afternoon, a justice of the peace and the few people who were still living in the area filled the barn to witness Absolom and Eleanor exchanging wedding vows. Absolom looked at Eleanor with such tender love in his eyes, Elly couldn't have been happier for her son. Eleanor looked like an angel in her peach dress and bonnet. She had been such a blessing since she arrived two months ago. She helped with the little ones, took over the sewing and the washing, and she could create delicious meals out of scraps. She was a very hard worker and always jumped in wherever she was needed, without ever being asked. She would be a good wife for Absolom and a good mother for their children.

During the ceremony, Elly stood next to James. He reached for her hand at one point and squeezed it. She looked up at him and smiled. On rare moments like this when the family was all together, life was good and all was right with the world. She refused to let the thought of Absolom and Eleanor moving away tarnish her happy mood.

The young couple repeated their vows after the justice, and then Absolom placed a ring on Eleanor's finger. Sarah stepped forward and sang the hymn "A Mighty Fortress is our God," with the small crowd singing along, and then James led the group in a prayer for a long and happy life for the newlyweds. At the very end of the ceremony, the justice asked Absolom to kiss his bride, and the onlookers exploded in applause and cheers.

During the applause, the celebration was interrupted by the caterwauling of Indians outside. The men jumped and ran toward the door, but the moment they reached it, it was slammed shut and blocked from the outside. The men pushed against it, but it wouldn't budge. They charged the door over and over, to no avail. What were the Indians doing?

"Momma," Jack cried and ran to his mother with his arms up. She bent down, picked up the toddler, and held him tightly.

"Lizzie!" she yelled for her daughter. "You and Sarah get the little ones and put them under the tables.

Thud. Thud. Thud. The sounds of arrows repeatedly hitting the barn walls. This confused Elly. Why would they shoot at walls? Elly's happiness turned to terror as she realized what was happening. They were locked in. There was no way out. And in horror, Elly realized those thuding arrows were armed with fire. Quickly, the smell of smoke and the crackling sound of burning wood filled the room. The barn was burning, and they were going to burn with it. Streams of smoke seeped into the barn through the seams of the walls and rose toward the ceiling, attempting to find an escape. She looked up, wondering if she could find an escape, too.

"James!" she screamed. Her husband was still pushing and pounding on the blocked door. "They're burning the barn! We have to find a way out!"

James turned toward Elly, and then followed her gaze upward and saw the smoke. Elly saw his face turn white, and the fear in his eyes frightened her more than the Indians and their fire-ladened arrows. Jack began to cry in her arms and she squeezed him tightly, whispering to him that everything would be all right, though she didn't know if that was the truth.

Absolom, who had watched the unspoken communication between his parents, bolted from the crowd of men at the door and headed for the ladder. He climbed onto the loft, where the window's shutters had been opened for the celebration. Elly knew he was going to climb out the upper window, but that window was more than fifteen feet off the ground.

"Absolom!" she yelled, but he didn't stop. He ran toward the open window.

"I'll jump, Momma."

Elly gasped. He would be killed jumping from that high up. And the Indians were out there. Her son was going to die trying to rescue his family. She couldn't breathe, not because of the smoke, but because fear paralyzed her as she watched her son disappear through the open window along with the rising smoke. Harvey, who was now fourteen, followed his older brother, but James yelled at him to stop.

Moments that seemed like hours later, the big barn door creaked and opened a crack. James and Hays pushed through it and bolted toward the house to retrieve their rifles.

Elly stood in the same spot in the middle of the barn, the roof now in flames. Bits of ash and spark dropped around her as she listened to the pop of gunfire outside. The roar of the flames intensified, and she yelled for the children to get out of the barn just as James appeared in the doorway with his rifle in hand.

"The Indians are gone. Everyone get out!" he yelled.

Elly, Lizzie, and Sarah ushered the younger children to safety. They pushed, coaxed, and carried the younger children all the way to the back of the yard. When all the little ones were accounted for, Lizzie approached her mother and took Jack from her arms. "Are you all right, Momma?"

Elly didn't answer. From the tree line, she had turned and was watching her barn burn to the ground. The black smoke against the sunny, blue sky looked like an ominous monster climbing upward. A monster that had almost killed them all.

"They actually tried to kill us," Elly mumbled, both disbelieving and terrified at the thought.

"I think so," Lizzie nodded and hugged Jack tighter.

Until now, the Indians had merely been a nuisance. They regularly stole livestock, and destroyed crops and property, but they had never before tried to hurt her family. The more the realization sank in, the angrier Elly became. The anger rose in her faster than the flames that were devouring her barn. She looked around for her husband and spotted him also standing near the tree line on the other side of the yard.

"James!" She hiked up her skirt and marched toward him, ready to let her temper fly. She was going to demand he pack their things into the wagons and move out of Creek territory this very moment.

"James!" She called him again, but he did not acknowledge her.

Suddenly, she realized how strange it was that he was just standing there ignoring her. He wasn't chasing the Indians. He wasn't putting out the fire. He remained stone still, staring at the ground. She followed his gaze and saw an unmoving leg on the ground. Then she noticed Eleanor kneeling and sobbing.

"Absolom!" She ran over and fell to her knees at his side.

"I'm all right, Momma." He grimaced, his back leaning against a large tree trunk. "I think I broke my leg when I jumped."

"How did you get the barn door open?"

"I crawled, Momma. I had to get you all out, so I

crawled."

Elly looked up at James just as Hays arrived and handed him a bed sheet. James ripped it into strips. He knelt down next to Absolom, placed a thick tree branch next to Absolom's leg, and asked Hays to hold it there. He wrapped the branch against the broken leg with the strips of cloth. Absolom winced with each touch and his face was turning white with pain. Elly took his hand, and gasped when she noticed his arm. An arrow was sticking out of his left bicep, and the sleeve around the wound was scorched.

"Hays, go for the doctor," Elly directed.

Hays nodded and ran toward the corral for the horse.

Eleanor sat across from Elly and held Absolom's other hand.

He looked into her eyes and whispered, "I'm sorry they ruined our wedding."

He fell unconscious.

LORI CRANE

No Accident

Eto ran into Tafv's house without knocking, out of breath, dripping from the pouring rain. When he entered, he found Tafv sitting at the table in the middle of the dim, musty smelling room.

Tafv looked up with surprise at the unannounced entrance.

"Tafv, the boy you shot with the arrow at the white man's house is still alive!"

"What? That can't be." Tafv shook his head. "I saw him fall from the barn window and I shot him through the chest."

"I know, I saw him, too, but the arrow didn't go into his chest. It went in his arm and he's still alive. I just saw him sitting in a chair on the front porch of their house."

Tafv let out a huge sigh of frustration. "I almost felt better knowing I had killed his son in retaliation for killing mine."

Eto lowered his voice. "You know Hasse Ola's death was an accident."

Tafv slammed his fist down on the table. The bowls that were resting there jumped and fell to the floor. One shattered, the other bounced across the floor. The racket made Eto jump. Tafv, his face turning red in anger, rose abruptly from his chair, knocking it over backward, and the crack it made when it hit the floor made Eto jump again.

Tafv stomped toward him, his jaw twitching in rage as he clenched his teeth. "No, Eto! It was no accident. It was no accident those people came here onto our land, it was no accident they built a house, and it was no accident they chased us down that night." He pointed in the direction of the family's house. "That white man chased us down on purpose and killed Hasse Ola. And I will have my revenge against him...sooner or later."

The two men stared at each other, apparently both surprised by the outburst.

Eto knew it was fate that killed Hasse Ola, but he also knew he would never be able to convince Tafv of that fact. The man was as stubborn as he was brave. Eto watched as Tafv eventually turned toward the overturned chair, picked it up, and placed it back where it was supposed to be. Tafv then sat back down and stared at the table.

Eto swallowed hard. He didn't move or say a word. He felt rainwater drip from his hair onto his face, tickling his nose, but he didn't wipe it away. In his thirty years, he had never seen his brother lose his temper. Eto had never witnessed such anger and wrath, and it was terrifying. Until this moment, he had always viewed his brother as nothing more than a brother and friend, but after this explosion of rage, he now understood why their enemies feared the mighty warrior.

After a few minutes, Tafv spoke again, but in a

calmer and quieter tone. "This will not be over until I kill one of his sons. Or maybe all of them."

He rose and stomped out the front door, almost knocking over Eto on his way out. Eto turned and watched his brother march across the road in the downpour, heading toward the woods. Eto hoped he wasn't going to the white family's home. If so, the whole family would be dead by morning.

1814 Joining the Militia

"They're under the command of Evan Austill," James explained. "He's a good man. He's been guarding Fort Glass for months. That's where a lot of settlers went after the Fort Sinquefield incident."

"Is that what you call it, an *incident*?" Elly frowned and continued drying the plate she held in her hand.

James ignored her comment and continued. "Evan is sending a party of volunteers southeast to take back control of the Alabama River. Hays said they have nearly seventy men, so the boys will be fine. The Indians will be greatly outnumbered."

Elly didn't respond.

"And the whole company will be fighting under Sam Dale. It's a large group of men, and that Sam Dale never lost a battle. Elly, you should be proud of Hays and Absolom."

She placed the last of the super dishes on the shelf in front of her and turned to face her husband. "Of course I'm proud of them. I just don't want anything to happen to them while they're off fighting some stupid war. I don't even understand who these Red Sticks are."

"The Red Sticks are the savages that destroyed Fort Mims. They got the name from painting their clubs red." James sipped his coffee. "I really don't think the boys will be in any danger. All the Indians have are clubs and tomahawks. They don't even have real weapons, and I don't think there's any way they could obtain any. The Mississippi Militia is a strong unit and Dale's battalion is supposed to be the best. Our boys won't be in any more danger fighting the Indians out there than we are fighting them right here." He sipped his coffee again. "And I don't think what they're fighting is a stupid war. They'll be protecting people like us from dangers like the massacre at Fort Mims and the *incident* at Fort Sinquefield. What the boys are doing is very important. Heck, if I was a younger man, I'd go join them."

"If you were a younger man, I'd expect you to." She stopped when she realized what she had said. Yes, her boys needed to go protect their neighbors and do right by their country. "I know it's right for them to go, and I know what they're doing is very important." She folded the dishcloth, placed it neatly on the counter, untied her apron, and slipped it off. "It's just that after Absolom was so severely injured, it upsets me to think something like that could happen to one of them out there, and I wouldn't be by their side. He's just now getting back to normal. It's taken two months. I'd hate for him to get hurt again."

James rose from the table and wrapped his arms around her waist. "Elly, you're a good mother, but you need to realize the children are growing up, and you have to let them go. Especially the boys. Hays is twenty-one now, and Absolom is eighteen and a married man. They're not little boys anymore, and they don't need their mommy watching out for them."

She looked into his warm brown eyes and appreciated that he was trying to calm her fears. "It doesn't matter how old they are. They'll always be my children."

He gently took the apron from her hands, placed it on the table, and kissed her on the forehead. "I know, and that's what I love about you. You're a fantastic mother and an amazing woman." He hugged her tightly.

"I miss them already, and they're probably going to be gone for months." She hugged him back, neither of them saying a word for a long time. Finally, she spoke again. "There's something else you don't know." She backed up from his embrace and looked up at him. "Eleanor's pregnant."

A big grin came to James's face, and what started as a small giggle turned into a huge roar of laughter.

"What are you laughing at?" She playfully pulled away from his hands around her waist.

"You. You're going to be a grandmother and have a whole new crew of children to worry about."

She narrowed her eyes at him.

"I'm just teasing you." He pulled her back into his arms. "You'll be a wonderful grandmother, and your sons will be home before you know it."

***

The next day, James and fourteen-year-old Harvey took a wagon full of corn to the gristmill to be ground into flour. The mill was located a few miles south of them, and James told Elly they would be back by the following morning. At most, the trip would take two days if the mill was backed up with customers.

After an hour of their absence, Elly felt as if they had already been gone a month. For some reason, she was jumpy and anxious, and had an awful premonition that something evil was looming on the horizon. Her mother always called that feeling mother's intuition. James called it being overprotective. Whatever it was, she couldn't shake it. Every time she turned around, she could have sworn she saw something, or *someone*, out of the corner of her eye. She knew it was only the uneasiness of her husband being gone. After twenty-three years of marriage, she was used to having him around all the time. She checked and double-checked the rifle on the mantel to make sure it was loaded. The Indians hadn't come around for a few weeks, but being without her husband and sons was making her feel extremely vulnerable. She was alone with six girls and the two youngest boys—Bo, now six, and Jack, now four. As she moved through her day and completed her chores, she kept eyeing the woods, and kept the children close.

Ambushed

Elly pushed a loose strand of hair from her face, and wiped the beads of sweat from her upper lip with the back of her hand. She placed a hand on her lower back and leaned back to ease the stiffness in her muscles. She rested her arm on top of her hoe and stood still for a moment to catch her breath. The morning sun was scorching, and though there were a few gray rainclouds in the sky, she knew it was going to be a sweltering afternoon. The humidity had risen greatly over the last day, and she hoped to get the garden planted before the day got too hot and the rain arrived. Just as she went back to work, the first rumble of thunder sounded. She looked up at the clouds, also hoping her husband and son would get back before the storms hit.

"We'd better hurry and get this done. It's going to rain soon."

"I'm trying to hurry, Momma, but it would help if Jack would stop trampling the tomato seeds," Sarah whined.

Jack laughed and ran in circles around them.

"Jack, behave yourself, or I'll give you a hoe and

put you to work," Elly chastised him in a teasing manner.

"He should have gone with Daddy and Harvey," Sarah added sarcastically. "When are they coming home?"

"Your father said probably this morning." Elly went back to hoeing.

Jack chased the chickens that were milling around, eating bugs unearthed by the hoes. Elly stopped hoeing when she heard a thud and a squawk from one of the chickens. It was a strange noise, and she looked over and saw the red hen lying on its side with an arrow through its breast. She yelled, "Get down!"

"What is it, Momma?" Sarah turned toward her mother.

Elly grabbed Jack by the arm and pulled him to the ground. "Indians! Get down!"

The moment the words escaped Elly's lips, Sarah clutched at her chest, for an arrow had buried itself there. Elly saw Sarah's eyes fill with panic as she collapsed to the ground.

"Sarah!" Elly crawled toward her daughter. She placed her hands on her daughter's chest, but the arrow had hit directly into Sarah's heart. She was gone.

Elly looked toward the woods and saw five Indians on horseback, holding bows in their hands. The one in the middle was the Indian she had seen many times—the one with the two feathers sticking up from his head. He sat tall and strong astride his enormous black horse, and he was covered in red and black paint, from the top of his head all the way down his bare chest. He was arming his bow, and for a moment, their eyes met. She froze for an instant, but she knew her children would be massacred if she didn't do something.

The back door of the house squeaked open and Lizzie looked out toward the garden. "What is it, Momma?"

Elly yelled, "Indians! Run!"

Lizzie disappeared into the house, and within seconds, Elly saw all her girls dash across the front yard.

Elly picked up Jack and headed in the same direction, passing the side of the house as an arrow whizzed past her head. She saw all the girls, but where was Bo? As she ran, she eyed the tree line and the horizon, but she didn't see him anywhere. Maybe he was still in the house. No, Lizzie wouldn't have left him. The family had previously discussed what to do in an Indian attack. Bo would not have been left in the house. Now that she thought about it, she hadn't seen Bo all morning. And what about Sarah? It broke her heart, but she knew there was nothing she could do for her daughter.

She clutched Jack in her arms and ran as fast as she could, crossing the front yard and the road. She stumbled and almost fell numerous times when she entered the field, getting tangled in her long skirt, but she kept moving. The Indians wouldn't kill a small child, would they? The children knew the best thing to do was scatter, according to their plan. She hoped they remembered what to do. She was relieved when she saw the girls split up. Lizzie ran straight ahead in front of her. Fifteen-year-old Susannah split from Lizzie and ran to the south. Seventeen-year-old Peggy ran to the north. Thirteen-year-old Ellie and eight-year-old Polly disappeared into the pine forest on the other side of the road.

"Jack, do you remember where I told you to hide?" Elly panted as she ran.

"Yes, Momma."

"I want you to go there now and be as quick and as quiet as a mouse. Don't come out until I come for you. It will probably be dark. You stay there no matter what."

"Yes, Momma."

She put him on the ground and pointed him toward the forest. "Go!"

The boy ran toward the hollowed out log that lay just inside the forest boundary. She watched him wiggle into the log. He would never be found there.

"God, take care of my babies," she whispered as she kept running through the overgrown field. The Indians were right behind her, closing in. She could hear their horses' hooves thumping on the dry ground toward her. Last year, James had dug a garbage pit, and she dove into it and covered herself in trash. The smell was atrocious; rotten vegetables, manure, broken bits of furniture, and unsalvageable pieces of clothing. She buried her head in the rubbish. The Indians rode right past her and then suddenly, the sound of the horses stopped. She hoped they weren't coming back, but why else would they have stopped? She didn't move, and she tried to stop panting by breathing slowly in and out of her nose. She listened for their return, but all she could hear was her own heart beating wildly in her ears. She knew she was shaking, but there was nothing she could do to stop herself. If the Indians looked into the pit, they would surely see her.

After a long continued silence, she slowly lifted her

head a few inches to look over the rim of the pit.

The Indians sat on their horses, facing away from her. She wondered if they would hear her if she crawled out of the pit. She wondered how long they would sit there, waiting for the family to return home. She watched a figure emerge from the trees and cross directly in front of the Indians' path. Then she realized it was an unsuspecting six-year-old boy with a fishing pole over his shoulder. Bo! Elly wanted to scream for him to run, but she couldn't utter a sound. Fear paralyzed her and constricted her throat. She watched Bo freeze when he saw the warriors in his path. His face turned as ashen as the rain clouds that were quickly filling the sky.

Time stood still. Bo dropped his fishing pole and turned to run. One of the Indians galloped up behind him, caught him by the shirt collar, and pulled him a foot off the ground. A second Indian jumped down from his horse, ran over to them, grabbed the boy by the hair, and ran his knife blade across the front of the boy's forehead.

They scalped him, dropped him on the ground, and left him for dead. Elly watched them gallop away, tears streaming down her face. She couldn't breathe. This couldn't possibly be happening.

The Indians hooted and hollered as they rode away, one of them waving the scalp of the young boy in circles above his head.

Elly watched her son for movement. There was none. Only moments ago, he was walking home. Now he was probably dead. The moment the Indians were out of sight, she crawled out of the pit and ran toward Bo, sobbing. It seemed she couldn't get to him. Everything was moving in slow motion, and every step seemed to take her farther away from him. The wind began to whip at her face and thunder boomed as her panic turned into terror.

When she finally reached him, she fell to her knees and rolled him over onto his back.

Heavy raindrops fell from the sky, landing on his pale face.

Thank God, he was still breathing.

She took off her apron, wrapped it around his bloodied head, and carried him home.

Murder

James and Harvey arrived back at the house later that evening. They were delayed because of the heavy rains, and rode through the puddles in the front yard. The first sight they saw when approaching the house was Elly sitting in a chair on the front porch with her rifle resting across her lap. She was covered head to toe in red dirt, with grime all over her face and what looked like trash in her hair. She also had large stains of something on her dress. She didn't rise to greet them as they approached. She stared across the road at the field and didn't say a word.

James pulled on the reins, bringing the horses to a stop right in front of the house. Cautiously, he said, "Elly?"

She didn't speak. She had never in two decades of marriage not greeted him. Something was seriously wrong.

He hopped down from the wagon, stepped over a puddle, and walked toward her. "Elly, what is it?"

She looked at him strangely.

"Elly?" He stepped up onto the porch and knelt down beside her chair. "What is it, honey?" She

147

smelled like manure. That is what was staining her dress.

"They've killed your daughter," she said flatly, turning to look at the mound under a blanket, lying on the grass to the right of the porch.

"What?" James followed her line of sight and saw the blanket for the first time.

"They attacked us. They killed Sarah and they scalped Bo."

James shook his head. She must be mistaken.

She raised her voice. "Don't shake your head at me. They killed your daughter and they scalped your son right in front of my face. I couldn't do anything to stop them."

James closed his eyes and shook his head again. It must be a bad dream. It must be. He had assured his wife they would be happy and safe here. He'd told her over and over the Indians would accept them.

"Elly, I..."

"Don't say another word, James." She glared at him.

"Where's Bo?"

"He's in his bed."

"Is he all right?"

"Well, except for missing the skin off the top of his head, sure, he's fine."

He stood up and looked between his wife, the blanket, and the front door of the house. After a moment, he walked over to the blanket and stared down at the bouquet of wild flowers lying on top of it. A tear fell, and he quickly wiped his eyes when he heard Elly approach him from behind.

"My place has always been with you, by your side," she said. "But I'm done with this. The moment Hays and Absolom are discharged from the militia, I am packing up my children and we are leaving this godforsaken place. You are welcome to come with us if you wish, but we are not staying here one moment longer than we have to."

James nodded.

Elly looked down at the blanket. "I will leave Sarah's body here in possession of the savages." She shoved the rifle into James's hand. "You need to guard your house and bury your daughter. I need to go inside and be with Bo. I don't know if he's going to survive what they did to him."

***

Elly didn't speak to James for the next week. She didn't speak to anyone. He tried to converse with her many times, but she always walked away, or stood mutely, or looked blankly over his shoulder. He couldn't get her attention, and he was worried. Sarah's death had devastated her, and Bo's condition was very slow in improving. The child had lost so much blood, he was still weak and horribly pale. Elly seldom left his side, and James worried about both of them. He prayed daily that he would not lose his son, and he desperately begged God that the love Elly had for him hadn't been destroyed. Maybe after she was done grieving Sarah and Bo got better, his smiling wife would eventually return. Maybe he could help her along. What if he showed these savages there were consequences for their actions? He could stop them from ever doing anything like this again. He could teach them a lesson. He could assure the safety of his family, and rebuild his relationship with his wife.

He decided he would go to the Indian village and confront the murderers. He was so angry about the years of raiding and theft and destruction and now death, he felt he could single-handedly slaughter all of them.

The following morning, he cautiously rode through the woods alone. Yesterday's storms had passed, but the wind was still whipping across the fields and through the trees, and the scattered clouds moved quickly across the sky. He wasn't sure what to expect when he reached the Indian village, but he knew at least one of them spoke English. He didn't know how he'd communicate if that person wasn't there, but he was sure he couldn't allow them to keep prowling around his property, frightening his wife, and killing his children.

As he neared the Indian village, he heard them before he saw them. Voices were clear over the wind whistling in his ears. He cautiously dismounted from his horse in the woods and continued on foot.

He had never seen an Indian village before. It was built in a square. Houses, more like mud huts, were lined up in perfect symmetry. A few women were milling around, carrying baskets and supplies from one place to another. Young naked children kicked a ball in a field that lay just outside the village. A large spot in the middle of the clearing held ashes from a gigantic fire. He wondered if they all cooked there, but then he saw chimneys on some of the roofs, so he didn't know what to make of the pit.

A woman dressed in a cape-like shirt and a long skirt emerged from the woods not far from James, and began to hang wet clothes on a line right in front of him. He had no doubt that if she turned, she would see him, so he backed up behind a large oak tree. To his left, a host of women worked in a large garden, but where were the men? He didn't see any. He wanted to speak with a man. He didn't know if they would be able to communicate through the language barrier, but was sure once they heard him speak, they would summon the Indian who spoke English.

He heard a twig snap in the woods to his left and he spun his head in that direction. A male Indian stood with a bow aimed in his direction. At that very moment, an arrow whizzed past James and buried itself in the large oak, about an inch above his head. Thank God for the strong winds or the bad aim of his assailant.

James grabbed his piston from his waistband and pulled the trigger. The single shot dropped the Indian instantly.

He felt his heart pounding and was relieved he would not die at the hands of that Indian, but his relief was only momentary, as he realized the sound of the pistol had alerted everyone in the village to his presence. Women and children scattered and he heard male voices coming in his direction. A few men emerged from houses, wildly looking around for the source of the gunfire. Women pointed in James's general direction. He turned and ran back to his horse.

The Indians were running toward him, and as he rode away, he heard a man's voice cry out, "Eto!"

He didn't know if *eto* meant *stop* or if that was the name of the man he had just shot, but he wasn't about to stick around and find out.

He rode like lightning all the way home, kicking his horse's sides with fury. He knew he hadn't remedied the situation, but probably made it worse.

***

He ran in the front door of the house in a panic, not even bothering to secure his horse on a picket or in the corral.

"What wrong with you?" Elly asked.

"I just shot an Indian!"

"You what?"

"I went to their village to confront them, and one of them shot an arrow at me, so I fired back and shot one. I think I killed him."

Elly threw the dishcloth down on the counter. "Why would you do something like that?"

"I thought I could make it better."

"By getting yourself killed? What are we supposed to do if they kill you?"

"I wasn't thinking about me, Elly." He paused and lowered his voice. "I was thinking about you."

"So, you killed an Indian because you were thinking about me? I don't understand."

"I was just trying to make it right, but I may have made it worse."

"Did they see you?"

"No, I don't think so, but who else would be over there with a gun shooting them?"

Elly sat down in the chair next to the table and rested her elbows on the table. She laced he fingers and leaned them against her chin. "I don't understand what this has to do with me," she said softly.

He walked over to her and fell to his knees in front of her. "I've been so worried about you since Sarah and Bo. I was afraid you'd never speak to me again."

"Well, I'm speaking to you now."

He laid his head in her lap and she ran her fingers through his hair.

"Elly, I'm so sorry for everything. You're right, the moment the boys are release from the militia, we'll go. I don't know where, but we'll go."

The joy she thought she'd feel when she finally convinced him to move did not come. It was too late. There was too much damage to the family. She gave him a weak smile. "Good," was all she could think of to say.

He looked up into her face. "How's Bo?"

She nodded. "He's doing better. He'll be all right. If his hair grows back in, you won't even be able to tell. If not, you'll have a bald son with a large scar across his forehead."

"As long as I have a son, hair or not."

***

Tafv picked his brother's body up from the leaf-covered floor of the forest and carried him, cradled like a baby, to his home across the field. Nearly twenty villagers followed behind, murmuring and crying, and at least a dozen men combed the forest for the killer, but they didn't find anything or anyone.

There was no need to search the forest. Tafv knew who did this.

Once he buried his brother and the appropriate

grieving time had passed, he would finish this once and for all

Hays and Marey

When Elly heard the horses approaching, she loaded her rifle and ran to the door, expecting the Indians, but when she opened the door, the sight before her was one of the best she had ever seen. Hays and Absolom were galloping toward the house. The moment they saw her waiting in the doorway, they both lit up with enormous smiles. Her heart beat wildly with excitement as she dropped the gun in the corner and yelled to her family, "Hays and Absolom are back! They're back!"

James came running from the side of the house with a hoe in one hand and a bucket in the other. He dropped them both on the side of the front porch when he saw his sons approaching. One at a time, the rest of the family appeared from various corners of the property. Harvey ran up and took the reins of both horses, patting them on their noses and smiling at his brothers. Bo hurried out onto the front porch, looking healthy except for the awkward patches of hair that had grown back unevenly.

Absolom jumped down first and patted Harvey on the shoulder. He then ran to the porch to greet his mother and his wife. He didn't know which one of the ladies to hug first, but when he saw his wife's protruding belly, he fell to his knees and hugged his unborn child first. The smile on Eleanor's face said all that everyone was thinking. The boys were home, everyone was overjoyed, and everything would be fine.

Hays hopped down from his horse and turned to help a young lady down from the back. Elly watched from the porch, wondering who the young lady was and why she was with them.

James reached for Elly's hand and they took a few steps out into the yard. Hays approached them arm-in-arm with the girl. He was beaming from ear to ear.

"Momma, Daddy, I'd like you to meet Miss Marey Scott."

James nodded at the girl and she shyly nodded back. She was a pretty young thing with eyes as blue as the sky and hair of deep coffee brown. Her eyes matched the bodice of her dress, which sat atop a flowing ivory skirt. Her smile was warm.

Elly reached for her hand. "It's very nice to meet you, Miss Scott."

"Oh, please call me Marey," the girl replied.

"Very well, Marey. Why don't we all go inside and have some tea, and you boys can tell us all about your adventures." Elly stuck her hand in the crook of Hays's elbow to allow him to escort her into the house. Marey and James followed behind, followed by Absolom, Eleanor, and the other children.

As Lizzie made tea for the family, everyone sat around the dining table and listened to Hays and Absolom tell heroic tales of brave soldiers and dead Indians.

"And then what happened?" asked Jack when Hays paused for a moment. Jack was sitting wide-eyed on Hays's lap.

"Then," continued Hays, "we swam to the other side of the river to escape."

No one in the room said a word. They were all waiting for the epic saga to continue.

Absolom jumped in at this point. "And we did escape, but our canoe was sunk. We were miles and miles away from anywhere, and we had no canoe, so we started walking, and when we'd gone a couple hundred yards, we heard a loud splash behind us in the river. We knew the Indians were pursuing us, so we climbed as fast as we could to the top of a steep hill. As much as Hays wants to make it sound like he was the hero,"—he punched Hays in the arm; Hays playfully rubbed his arm and rolled his eyes—"when we got to the top of the hill, he turned around to see if the Indians were still chasing us. And they were! We heard them coming through the brush, though we couldn't see them. Hays backtracked a ways and ducked down under the bottom of the tree branches to try to get a better look, but when he did so, he lost his shoe and tripped and rolled almost the whole way back down the hill."

Jack's eyes were now as big as saucers.

Elly interrupted. "Are you sure this story is suitable for the young ones?"

Hays smiled, nodded at his mother, and Absolom continued.

"We all turned and loaded our guns, knowing Hays had caused us to get in the middle of a battle. We followed him down the hill, running as fast as we could in an effort to save him, but when we got down there, there wasn't an Indian in sight. We turned around and around, searching for the Indians, when suddenly a big herd of deer jumped out of the trees and ran straight toward us. There must have been fifteen or twenty of them. We all jumped behind trees to avoid getting flattened like flapjacks. Turns out, we were being chased by deer, not Indians."

After the family had a good laugh, Hays continued. "I did eventually find my shoe, and we headed back down to the river and walked the rest of the way to camp. It was a long, long day."

Marey giggled at the mishap, and Elly looked at her. "So, Marey, where do you fit into this story? How did you end up with these silly boys?"

Marey glanced at Hays and blushed. Elly looked at Hays, too. "Or maybe you'd like to tell us, Hays."

He grinned at his mother, and she knew exactly what was coming next. Her son was in love with this pretty girl, and if they weren't already married, they would be soon.

"Well, it happened like this," Hays began. "Absolom and I were on our way to Fort Glass and we needed a place to stay the night. We holed up in a barn, and at daybreak, we were caught by the farmer who owned it. He wasn't upset at us for sleeping in his barn. As a matter of fact, he was very kind and offered us a hot breakfast before we left." He gestured with his hand to Marey. "And this is the young lady who made us that breakfast."

They smiled at each other while Elly, James, and the rest of the family looked back and forth between the two of them.

Absolom jumped in. "I knew they liked each other the moment they met. Hays didn't even eat any breakfast because he spent the hour staring at Marey. You know something is amiss when Hays doesn't eat breakfast."

Elly laughed. Marey glanced at Absolom and smiled.

Elly asked, "But wait. That was on your way *to* Fort Glass? That was months ago. How did you end up here, Marey?"

Marey opened her mouth to answer but Absolom beat her to it. "When we left the farm after breakfast, Hays told me, 'I'm gonna marry that girl.' I laughed at him, but darn it all if he didn't convince me to go with him to visit that same farm on the way home."

"Well, I guess I don't need to tell the story now, little brother, but long story short, we stayed at the farm for a couple days and I won Marey's heart."

"Eh, it's always more interesting when I tell the stories," Absolom teased.

Elly looked across the table at Marey, who was sipping her tea. "So, Marey, I gather you're here to stay?"

"Yes, ma'am, if you'll have me."

Elly walked around the table and gave the girl a hug. "Of course we will."

When the two women sat back down, Hays announced, "We'd like to get married as soon as possible."

Elly looked at Lizzie and asked, "Would you mind having two weddings this month?"

"Of course not," Lizzie grinned.

Absolom and Hays looked from their mother to their sister, wondering what they were talking about.

Elly explained, "Lizzie has met a nice young man named Jesse Landrum, and they're getting married on the twenty-ninth."

Hays smiled at his sister. "Congratulations, Lizzie. I hope we get to meet this Mr. Landrum soon."

"I'm sure you will, Hays. He's probably coming around tonight or tomorrow to get things ready for the wedding." Lizzie blushed.

Hays turned his attention back to his mother. "Momma, we certainly don't want to get in the way of Lizzie's wedding, but we need to do this as soon as possible. Marey's pa wasn't too happy with her taking off with me and Absolom, so I promised I would make an honorable woman of her the moment we got here."

"Oh." Elly was surprised by the rush, but if that's what they had to do, so be it. "All right, then. We'll see if the justice can come out tomorrow."

***

Hays and Marey married the next day in a small ceremony with only the family present, and the Indians didn't ruin the wedding this time.

Two weeks later, Lizzie and Jesse married, but when their ceremony was over, they set out in Jesse's wagon to move closer to his family in Grove Hill, which was a couple days ride from Elly's home. Elly's heart was heavy. She hated to see her firstborn move away.

Within a few months, Elly's spirits were lifted when Eleanor gave birth to the very first grandchild. She was named Eleanor Margaret Rodgers. Elly couldn't have been more pleased to have a little one in the house again, especially a cute little girl, and she pampered and fawned all over the baby. Her happiness didn't last, however, as shortly after the birth, Absolom packed up his wife and child and followed Lizzie and Jesse to Grove Hill.

Deep inside, Elly was happy for her children. She was happy they'd found love and were having their own children, and living their lives the way God intended, but she was so unhappy to lose them from her daily life, and even sadder to lose her first granddaughter. Fortunately, within a few months, Marey announced she was with child, and Elly spent the spring and summer making plans for her new grandchild.

***

Through that year, the family fought the Indians almost daily. The damage and theft wasn't severe, but it was constant. One day they would find some of their animals killed, the next, they would find property missing or destroyed, the following, their field of crops flattened. One morning, one of their mares was gone, and this morning, Elly couldn't find a couple of her chickens. That was the hardest to deal with—when the Indians stole the animals the family used for food, or destroyed their crops. Feeding the children was a constant uphill battle. Every time a harvest of fruit trees or berries was about to come in, Elly would find the tree cut down or the bushes dug up. She was at her wit's end.

Enough time had passed since anything violent happened that she was no longer afraid of the Indians killing her family, but she was still cautious of them and their marauding, and counting down the days until Hays was discharged from the militia so they could move away. She heard the western part of the Mississippi Territory was not so dangerous. The Choctaw Indians lived there, and they were a peaceful nation, unlike the Creeks who surrounded her. Oh, how she longed for peace. She wanted to move west. She wanted to live in a place where she knew she could feed her children without such a struggle, and she wanted to stop looking over her shoulder for Indians lurking in the trees. She was weary of the nightmares she had every night about the Indian with the two feathers sticking up from the back of his head. It had become a nightly ritual for her to wake up in a cold sweat and not be able to fall back to sleep, and then carry that same sense of dread the rest of the day.

She still needed to talk to her husband and decide where to move to, and she wondered if she could convince Lizzie and Absolom to uproot their families and come along, too.

Causing Trouble

It had been a chilly drizzle all day, and the gray evening clouds hung heavy with the promise of more of the same throughout the night. The weather matched Tafv's mood. He was weary and his heart heavy, and his future also promised more of the same. Day after day, the sadness did not ease. He wondered if he would ever emerge from this dark cloud he was now living under.

Hillis Hiya approached him, stepping over puddles in the village square, his arms holding his coat closed against the cold breeze. "Mekko wants to know what you're doing."

Tafv had placed a woven blanket on his black steed and was attaching knives and tools to it. He usually rode bareback, but today was different.

"Tell him I'm going to run the white family off our land once and for all."

Thunder boomed, making both men look at the sky. "Now? Tonight?"

"Yes, tonight. We're going to kill the last of their animals and destroy their remaining crops. We will leave nothing, and when they get hungry, they'll leave."

"You've been trying to get them to leave for almost four years now. Why don't you just kill them all and be done with it?"

Tafv stopped his preparation and turned to face Hillis Hiya. The muscle in his jaw twitched. "We've been killing white men for decades, we killed hundreds of them at Fort Mims, and it hasn't done any good. More and more of them keep coming. If we make it impossible for them to live here, they will spread the word, and they will stop coming." Tafv returned his focus to his horse. "And besides, this family is different. We've done everything we can do to them, and they just won't leave. I think we have to run them out by starving their children."

Hillis Hiya thought about that for a moment and shrugged. "Yes, maybe you're right."

"Tell Mekko I've rounded up a dozen braves and we're going to take care of this."

Tafv hopped up onto his horse with the ease of a child jumping over a puddle. "Tell him we'll be back before sunrise." Tafv turned his horse to the left and kicked it in the ribs.

He galloped off as Hillis Hiya yelled after him, "Good luck!"

Tafv kept tight control over his prancing steed as he went door to door to gather his men. Then they headed to the white man's farm under the cloak of darkness, and destroyed every crop in the field and the family's garden. They used hatchets on the berry bushes, pulled up the vegetables by the roots, broke off limbs of fruit trees. Then they killed every animal except the oxen and horses. They left the oxen to pull the white man's wagon, and took the horses with them.

"With the long winter looming and no food to store, they will have to leave. They'll have no choice. This is finally finished," Tafv mumbled to himself as he rode back to his village with the first ribbons of morning light streaking through the gray rain clouds.

Hunger and Baby Lewis

When James reentered the house only moments after he had left, Elly knew something was wrong. "What have they done now?" she asked, accustomed to the daily mischief caused by the Indians.

"What *haven't* they done, is more like it." James walked toward the fireplace.

"What do you mean?" She set down her coffee cup and rose from the table to look out the back door.

James retrieved his rifle from the mantel. "Keep the children inside for the morning while we clean up this mess."

"What mess? What have they done?" she asked as she opened the door, but he was already disappearing down the hall to wake Hays and Harvey and didn't answer her.

She stepped out into the cloudy first light of morning, and the massacre that lay before her took her breath away. There was blood everywhere. Dead animals were strewn about like rag dolls, covered in mud and blood. Off in the corner of the yard, two foxes tore apart what was left of one of her chickens.

She clapped her hands at them and yelled and they ran off. Flies were swarming about the remains. She placed her hand over her mouth in horror as she stepped over one of her goats lying at the bottom of the steps. She was shocked that the Indians had gotten that close to her house without anyone hearing them. She walked over to the hog pen. The hogs were dead, cut into pieces. Blood was smeared on the posts and the rails of the fence. A second goat lay by the open gate of the hog pen. She glanced out into the field, but didn't see any sign of her cow. There would be no milk for the children if the cow was dead, too. More shocking than not seeing her cow was the flat field that lay before her. The six-foot-tall cornstalks were all gone, flattened. The wheat wasn't there. She walked around the barn to check her vegetable garden. The peas and onions were gone, the tomato plants trampled into the muddy ground, the pumpkins smashed. The berry bushes were gone. The apple tree was destroyed. There was nothing left. How would they make it through the winter?

James appeared behind her. "We'll clean this up, Elly."

She turned toward him. "We need to pack up and go."

"Well, we can't do that today." He strolled past her, not breaking stride for the puddles or for her demands.

"And why not?" She put her hands on her hips and watched him walk away.

"Because your daughter-in-law has just gone into labor."

"Marey's having the baby?"

"Apparently." He marched toward the barn. "I'll

keep Hays busy today."

Elly went back into the house and spent the day delivering her first grandson, Lewis.

Militia Discharge

Hays, his again-pregnant wife, Marey, and his nine-month-old son, Lewis, sat at the breakfast table enjoying the first of the fall harvest. It had been a long, hungry winter for the family, followed by a very dry summer, and they had all lost a lot of weight over the nine months. Hays routinely gave most of his portions to Marey, but he often worried about how thin his mother had become, for he knew she was doing the same for the younger children with her portions. She resembled a starving animal, as her eyes had lost their sparkle and seemed to have sunken into her head. His father wasn't much better. If Hays had to bet, he would have wagered his dad had lost at least thirty pounds. They struggled through the winter and dry summer as best they could, and the harvest brought promise of a brighter future. The crisp weather brought forth a healthy yield of tomatoes, potatoes, and onions, and the corn and wheat would be harvested within a few short weeks. As they ate, Hays made silly faces at baby Lewis, who gave his father roaring belly laughs. The more the baby laughed, the more animated Hays became. He shoveled big, plump tomatoes into his mouth, making his cheeks balloon. When he bit down, the juice squirted out his mouth, dribbling down his chin. The baby's laughter filled the house.

In between Hays's antics with the baby, he and Marey exchanged small talk over the tomatoes and coffee. James opened the squeaking back door, popped his head inside, and interrupted the family's bonding. "Hays, there's a militia man here to see you."

"A militia man?" Hays looked at his wife questioningly, and her expression was not a happy one. Her face revealed her fear that the militia soldier was there to take Hays back into service. She let out a faint grunt as she awkwardly rose from the chair. She held Lewis on her hip.

Hays wiped his fingers on his trousers as he held the door open for his wife to exit first. She emerged onto the porch with their son in her arms and warily eyed the young soldier standing in the yard. Hays squinted in the morning light as he stepped off the porch and approached the soldier standing beside his chestnut mare.

"Yes, sir, how may I help you?"

"Are you Private Hays Rodgers?" The man took a step toward him and held out his hand.

"Yes, sir, I am." Hays shook the man's hand.

Elly approached the group from around the side of the house, wiping her hands on her apron. She stood next to James and glanced up at Marey on the porch. She raised her eyebrows to Marey, but Marey only shrugged.

The soldier reached into his jacket pocket, pulled out a folded paper, and held it out toward Hays. "I have your discharge certificate here, Private Rodgers."

"Discharge?"

"Yes. Your commitment is over and the militia is releasing you from duty."

Hays reached for the paper and unfolded it. He read it as his parents and wife waited with anticipation. Slowly a smile formed on his lips.

"Is it true, Hays?" his wife asked.

"Yes. Yes, it is." He turned toward her and read aloud. "It says, 'The bearer hereof Hays Rodgers, a private in Captain Evan Austill's company of volunteers in Major Sam Dale's battalion, having served since February 1814, his term of service having expired on the 7th of October 1818, is entitled to an honorable discharge. He has been paid up to the 31st day of August 1818, has returned his arms and accoutrements in good order, and has received his full allowance of clothing. He is entitled to pay from the 31st day of August 1818, together with three months' pay as his allowance upon being honorably discharged, along with pay and rations from this place to his place of residence in Clarke County, Mississippi Territory.'"

As he read, Elly walked up next to him to look over his arm at the paper.

He turned toward her. "I've been discharged, Momma." He wrapped his arms around her waist, picked her off the ground, and spun her in a circle. He gently placed her back down when he realized she was nothing but skin and bones, and he worried for a moment he might break her ribs if he wasn't more careful.

She smiled at Hays and held on to her straw gardening hat as he placed her down. She then turned to the militia soldier. "What about Absolom? Do you have a certificate for Absolom Rodgers?"

The soldier nodded as he pulled another folded paper from his jacket pocket. "Yes, indeed, I am also looking for Private Absolom Rodgers."

Hays held out his hand for the paper. "He's my brother. I'll give it to him."

The soldier, seemingly pleased that he did not have to roam the countryside looking for Absolom, handed Hays a second folded paper. "Very well, sir." He mounted his mare and tipped his hat to the ladies. "Have a good day, everyone."

The family watched the soldier ride off, and the moment he was out of sight, they erupted in hoots and hollers, kisses and hugs. The crisp, sunny morning, the promise of a decent harvest, and the good news had everyone smiling.

"We'll have a celebration tonight!" Elly declared. She looked at James. "Then we'll begin packing."

"Packing?" Hays looked at his mother.

"We'll talk about this later, Elly."

Hays looked to his father for an explanation, but James shook his head, declaring the conversation over.

Hays and James immediately set out on a hunting expedition to supply the family with game for the party. They bagged a small deer, and that evening, the family had a great celebration.

Elly and Tafv

The next morning, Elly rose early and entered the barn in the dim hours before any of her family was awake. She lit a lantern on one of the tables and wrapped her sweater tightly around her. She looked around, wondering where to start. It was a simple task that needed to be done, but she was torn. She needed to clean up last night's celebration dishes, but she wanted to wash them and pack them in the wagon, not place them back in the kitchen cupboard. She stood and stared down at the table as she thought about the last five-and-a-half years.

They had been a nightmare. She had lost one child to the Indian savagery, and almost lost Absolom and Bo, too. Her boys had gone to fight in a war against the Indians. Two of her children had moved away because of the Indians. She couldn't understand why her husband still called this place home. In her mind, this was only a temporary holding spot for her belongings, where she was forced to remain until the boys were released from duty. Now that that had happened, she didn't want to stay any longer than she had to. Why take the chance of the Indians harming more of her family members? It was time to go.

She started to stack the dishes to get them washed, then stopped and wondered where they would move to. She and James had discussed it many times, but they had never made a firm decision as to where they would move. He had agreed to a move once the boys were discharged, but she thought she would have to twist his arm to get him to actually pack and go. He certainly wouldn't go back to Tennessee and admit defeat. Besides, there was no house to go back to. The East and the South weren't any better than here. The Indians were fighting all around them, and settlers were being killed everywhere. That left only one place—unchartered pioneer territory in the West. Would her family be safe there? Elly didn't know for sure, but she had heard the Choctaw Indians in the West were friendly. Then again, James thought the Creek Indians would be friendly, too.

She shook her head in frustration and resumed stacking the dirty dishes. She placed them in a basket and carried them down to the creek. She could easily fetch a basin of water and wash them at home, but she really wanted to get away for a while and think. She needed a plan before she spoke with James, and the babbling creek always seemed to clear her head and help her organize her thoughts.

The stroll through the crisp pines was refreshing. The leaves were just beginning to fall and the air smelled delicious. The morning songbirds accompanied her on her journey. She watched a squirrel cross her path and followed his movement to a large black walnut tree. She looked around at the deep green of the pines, and the rich golds and yellows of the trees, with the morning light filtering sideways through the bushes and tree trunks. She noticed the sun casting its rays on the mist in front of her. James was right about one thing—it sure was beautiful here. Yes, she would miss this land, but she would not miss the Indians. To her left, a large buck stared at her, then darted onto the trail in front of her and hopped toward the creek. She watched his white tail bob up and down until it disappeared. As she neared the babbling creek, she breathed in the cool damp mist.

She knelt on the bank and unpacked the dishes from the basket, placing them on the large boulders. As she rinsed them, the water felt cold on her hands, but she didn't mind it. She listened to a frog singing his song only for her, then strangely, she could have sworn she heard a horse snort as it exhaled. She looked around for the source of the sound. It may have been the buck, but she thought for sure it was a horse. She spun her head left and right but saw nothing, so she focused back on stacking the dishes. She heard a twig snap. She looked up and caught movement in the trees in front of her, across the water. She stood up to get a better look.

Almost like ghosts, they moved silently through the trees, no fewer than a dozen Indians. They were traveling on horseback in a straight line toward the creek—directly toward her. They all wore different headdresses, most wore shirts, a few didn't, but they all wore red and black war paint on their faces. They held bows, axes, and tomahawks. As they moved closer to her, she wondered momentarily where they were going, then realized the only thing that lay behind her was her house, where her family still slept.

She turned and ran to alert her family, but after a

few steps, she heard the horses splashing across the creek, coming directly at her. She breathed heavy. Her heart pounded in her ears. She heard a small cry and realized it came from her own mouth. She looked around the woods as she ran, but there was no place to hide, nowhere to run, no way to escape them, no way to warn her family. She could hear the hooves pounding, increasing to a gallop. They were right behind her. If she stopped running, she would be trampled. Within seconds, the horses closed in on her.

A shrill shout broke the morning stillness, sending a wave of fear through her entire body. The lone Indian cry was followed by more in kind as they hollered their war whoop. She stopped and bent over, throwing her hands up to her ears to block the sound, and she braced herself for being crushed by the mighty horses. She knew she would be dead within a few short moments. If the horses didn't crush her, the Indians would surely grab her by the hair and scalp her, like she saw them do to Bo. Either way, she hoped it would be quick.

The horses grazed her as they galloped past on either side, and the dust from the ground billowed up around her, invading her nostrils and making her cough. The horses kept going, and she peeked up from her crouch to see them.

When she realized she was still alive, she wiped the dust from her face. She slowly stood up straight and watched the last of them ride away, their horses' hooves beating the ground like drums, their war cries ringing through the trees. Why did they not kill her? But they were still headed toward her house. She glanced from one side of the trail to the other, trying to think of a way to cut them off and get to her family first, but there was no shortcut. Determination overcame her fear, and she decided to run as fast as she could through the trees and fight them with her bare hands if necessary, anything to keep them away from her family.

She hadn't taken more than two steps when she was grabbed from behind. A muscular arm was around her waist, pinning her right arm to her side, and another arm was wrapped around her neck. She reached her free left hand over her head and groped at her assailant. She grabbed a handful of something and pulled with all her might. It easily came loose in her hand and she held it in front of her eyes. It was two feathers held together with deer hide and beads. It was him. The one who thought James had murdered his son. The one who had tortured her family for years.

She struggled to pull free, shrieking like a wild animal, but the man's massive arms were unyielding. It was as if she was fighting a rock. Somehow, he quickly pinned both of her wrists behind her back in one of his large hands. When she felt the cold blade of a knife at her throat, she froze.

The Indian didn't make a sound, but she could feel his chest rising against her back with each breath he took. She heard him breathing in her ear.

Her emotions quickly changed from rage to fear to sorrow. She held her head back against him, stretching her neck away from the blade. Her eyes welled with tears.

She was going to die in the hands of this savage. She was going to leave her children without a mother, her husband without a wife. The thought broke her heart, but at least her fear and pain would be gone. Her husband and children would probably die today also, so they wouldn't have to face the loss. The Indian behind her, however, would still have to face his pain every day—the pain of losing a child. If his heart was as crushed as hers was from losing Sarah, he lived with great sorrow that would never go away.

"I'm sorry," she murmured.

The Indian stood as still as stone.

Elly could feel his hot breath on her ear. Was he going to speak?

She waited.

He said nothing.

"I don't know if you can understand me," she began, "but my husband did not kill your boy. It was an accident. He would never kill a child. He loves children. And murdering my family will not bring your son back." She began to sob.

Tafv loosened his grip slightly but still held her firm.

He does understand me, Elly realized.

"I'm sorry about your son. I too have lost a child. I know how much it hurts."

She was shaking now, not only from fear, but the racking sobs.

They were both startled by a scream coming from the direction of the house. She looked up and saw black smoke billowing above the tree line, and heard the sounds of male and female voices yelling, mingling with the sounds of the Indians howling and shrieking. They were burning her house! She strained against her captor's grasp, but he held her tight. The Indians' caterwauling silenced when gunfire rang out—again and again. Within moments, the sound of horses' hooves grew, and she knew the Indians were heading back toward them. The man holding her did not move.

She saw the Indian's horses coming through the woods toward her, and when they approached, they abruptly stopped, eyeing Elly and the man holding her. They shouted something that Elly didn't understand. The Indian behind her responded in a rough but controlled tone, and then the others rode on without another word.

The man holding her relaxed his grip on her wrists and released the knife from her throat, and she cautiously turned around to face him. They stared at each other for a long time. His intense black eyes behind his red war paint were the most beautiful eyes she had ever seen, taking her breath away. They were mesmerizing pools of wisdom, of agony, of camaraderie. His face was filled with a deep compassion and she was in awe, almost melting into him. Despite their private war, she felt a startling and unexplainable connection to this warrior—a connection through despair, loss, and pain. But somehow, she knew he had lost more than she even had to lose.

Finally the Indian looked down at the ground, breaking their connection. What Elly saw in that moment surprised her. The warrior in front of her was a broken man. Though he was large and powerful and nearly impenetrable, his slumped shoulders told a story of sorrow. She felt a compassion that she never thought she would feel for any Indian, especially this one. He was just a man—a father who had lost his child, and probably more.

Elly stepped back a foot and slowly raised her arm.

She opened her palm and held out the two feathers she was still gripping. He looked at her hand, then back into her eyes. He slowly reached up and gently took the feathers from her hand, and she collapsed to the ground. Her legs would not hold her weight any longer. She was overcome by what had transpired between them and the pain she saw in the man's eyes. She bowed her head in respect. She didn't know if the Indian would kill her now, and she gasped when he softly touched the top of her head. She looked up at him and he quickly removed his hand. He spun around and walked toward his giant black horse. He jumped up in one fluid movement, kicked the animal in the ribs, and galloped away without looking back. Elly watched him cross the creek, and kept staring until he was out of sight.

The Fire

Elly shook her head in an attempt to erase the pain she experienced in the Indian's eyes. She knew her family back at the house was in trouble, but she found it hard to tear her eyes away from the other side of the river. She took a deep breath and shakily rose to her feet. When she found her legs were strong enough, she turned and ran toward the smoke.

The moment she emerged from the woods, she stopped dead in her tracks. Her home was completely engulfed in flames that were shooting high into the air, and menacing black smoke was billowing into the blue sky. James and Hays stood near the house holding empty water buckets. They stared at the house, knowing the battle was over. Their feeble attempt at putting out the fire had been no match for the monster devouring their every possession. Elly couldn't move. She stared at the flames, and then she remembered the children. She scanned the area, and saw her daughters and young Bo huddled on the ground, all sobbing and holding each other. She hurried toward pregnant Marey, who was standing behind the children. As Elly walked toward them, glancing over her shoulder at James and Hays, she wondered where Harvey was. The answer soon became clear. The children weren't merely huddled together, they were huddled around something.

Elly screamed, "No!"

She lifted her skirt and ran toward them. Peggy and Susannah looked up as she neared.

"Momma," Peggy whimpered, her cheeks tearstained.

On the ground, in the middle of the group, lay Harvey, an arrow piercing his chest.

"He's going to die, Momma," cried Peggy.

Elly fell to her knees next to the boy. She heard herself sobbing above the roar of the flames as she placed her head on his chest. Then she felt a faint heartbeat. "He's not going to die. Go get the doctor! Hurry!" she commanded Peggy and Susannah.

She sat upright and looked over at James and Hays, both still unmoving, gazing at the last of the burning house. The one remaining wall collapsed, and Hays jumped at the noise. James didn't move.

"Stay with Harvey," she told Marey as she rose to her feet.

She marched toward James, determined to leave this godforsaken place this very minute. James could come with her or not, but she was taking her children and leaving—leaving the destruction, the death, the savages who had destroyed her life.

"James!" she said sharply.

He continued to stare at the flames.

When she reached him, she saw tears streaming down his face, creating white stripes in the black soot that covered him. But she was not going to back down—not this time.

"We're leaving," she stated.

He did not answer.

"Do you hear me, James? We're packing and we're leaving—now."

He looked down at her as if he didn't recognize her, his eyes searching hers for some semblance of reality. "There's nothing left to pack," he said.

"James, you need to go over there,"—she pointed toward the children—"and take care of Harvey."

"Why? What happened to him?"

"He's injured. These savages you assured me would become our friends have almost killed another of your children."

James's face snapped from sadness to disbelief to anger as he looked toward the crying children huddled by the trees.

"Oh, no," he whispered. He looked back at Elly. "I'm sorry, Elly. I'm sorry for everything."

He turned and ran toward the children.

Elly wanted to soothe him, but she was beyond emotion. The last hour of terror, grief, and now anger was too much for her to bear. She couldn't allow another emotion to surface or she might go insane.

She marched to the barn and began packing up what was left of their lives.

Victory or Defeat

The next morning was shaded by a cloudy sky. The rising sun had turned the clouds red, and Tafv knew rain would come very soon. He sat atop his massive black horse, high on the bluff, and watched the Rodgers family roll away beneath him. They had arrived with eleven children. They were leaving with fewer. From what he understood, some of their children had married and moved away, and at least one had died at the hands of his band of warriors. He felt bad for them, but he had suffered great loss also. Nila had died at the hands of a white man. Hasse Ola's young life had been ripped from him by this white man. And his best friend and brother, Eto, had also been killed by a white man's gun, probably belonging to the man below him.

When Hasse Ola died, Tafv had vowed revenge against these people and had now succeeded in running them off his land, but he didn't feel any better for it. In the words of the white woman, murdering them would not bring his son back. Nothing would ever do that. Scalping every white man in the territory would not bring his family back, and it would certainly never reclaim his people's way of life. That was gone forever.

He watched the wagons until they were completely out of sight.

He rode down from the bluff and returned to his village. He went straight to the Great Chief's house to report the outcome. He was ushered into the house by the beautiful Talisa, who looked at him with great concern and touched his shoulder. He looked down into her dark eyes and was moved by the warmth he saw there. He gave her a small smile.

"I never got the chance to tell you how sorry I am about Hasse Ola and Eto."

"Thank you."

The Great Chief emerged from behind the woven curtain.

"Tafv!" he said. "Any word of the white family?"

Tafv tried not to look at Talisa as she helped her grandfather into his chair at the head of the table.

"Yes, Mekko, they are finally gone."

"That is good news. Congratulations. Sit down, and tell me all the details."

Tafv sat at the table as Talisa excused herself and walked out of the room. He then told the Great Chief about the encounter, including the burning of the white man's house and his confrontation with the white woman.

"It sounds like you accomplished what you wanted to."

Tafv hung his head and didn't respond.

"You don't look very happy, Tafv. What is it?"

He looked at the Great Chief. "What good does any of it do?"

"It does a lot of good. We have reclaimed what is

rightfully ours. We have shown the white man once again that this is our land, a gift of the Great Spirit, and they are not welcome here."

"But something happened to me out there that I don't understand. When I looked into that woman's eyes, I saw an empathy and compassion. I've never encountered a person that strong before—certainly not a woman. I exacted my revenge and destroyed her family, just as they destroyed mine, but I'm not happy about it. And this is not over. There'll soon be another white family arriving on their heels."

"Probably, but we'll deal with those as they come."

Tafv traced the grain of the wood on the table with his thumb. "And what do I do about my life? Hasse Ola's dead. Eto's dead. I don't think Nila would be very proud of me." He shook his head. "I'm not proud of myself."

"You can't keep everyone safe. And you can't single-handedly stop the ways of the world. I know you want to preserve our way of life, but maybe some things are not able to be preserved. Perhaps we need to consider embracing some of the white man's ways and merging them with our own. It may be the only way to preserve our heritage."

Tafv didn't agree, so he said nothing.

"You are a brave and valiant warrior, but maybe you have to pick and choose your battles and not try to fight the whole world."

"I did choose my battle. I chose to raise Hasse Ola in a manner Nila would have been proud of." Tafv scowled at the Great Chief.

Mekko sighed. "And you did the best you could, but they are both gone now."

Tafv looked back at the lines on the table.

"Tafv, you don't want to hear this, but it's time to let them go. Do not hold their spirits here with your sorrow. You need to allow them to be free. You need to allow yourself to be free."

"I know you're right, Mekko. Wise as always. I just don't know how to rebuild my life from here. I feel like I'm starting all over with no foundation to build upon."

"The first thing you need to do is stop ignoring the maidens who want to take care of you."

"I'm not interested in them." He knew the Great Chief was right, but he didn't know if he was ready to allow someone into his life at this point.

Mekko drank from his cup and placed it back down on the table decisively. "We will have a celebration at the next full moon and invite all the neighboring villages. You will take a wife. You will find one at the powwow."

Tafv reluctantly nodded.

The Great Chief continued. "I will make sure Talisa is there."

Tafv looked at the Great Chief, surprised. He then rose and bowed as he backed out the doorway.

He stopped on the porch and looked across the village square at the people working and conversing. He found it strange that they continued with their daily lives as if nothing had happened, when his life had come to a complete stop a few years ago. He knew he needed to rebuild it, and perhaps that started with taking a new wife. Perhaps it meant having more children. Perhaps the world he would bring them into would be a better world.

THE END

Epilogue

In 1818, the Rodgers family moved west and settled in Lauderdale County, Mississippi, in the land of the friendly Choctaw Indians. Eight years later, James died in Mississippi at the age of fifty-nine on August 9, 1826. Following his death, Elly moved back to Alabama to live either with her daughter Lizzie or with her son Absolom.

Lizzie and her second husband, Thomas Matlock, eventually moved to Texas and are buried in Glenwood Cemetery in Houston County.

Absolom and Eleanor Rodgers remained in Clarke County, Alabama, and had eight children. They both died in Grove Hill, Clarke County, Alabama, in 1853.

Hays and Marey Rodgers remained in Lauderdale County and had fourteen children. They both died of typhoid fever the winter of 1862-1863.

In 1830, the Treaty of Dancing Rabbit Creek forced the Indian nations to forfeit their lands to the United States government, and most of the Indians were relocated to the Oklahoma Territory, where the Creek Nation is still present to this day.

Elly Hays Rodgers died in Grove Hill, Clarke County, Alabama, in the 1830s. The exact date of death is unknown. Her burial place is unknown.

Author's Notes

The speech by Tecumseh in the opening chapter of this book is from *Life and Times of Gen. Sam Dale, the Mississippi Partisan* by Claiborne, J.F.H., New York: Harper and Brothers, 1860. Pages 59-61. It was reported to J.F.H. Claiborne by General Samuel Dale, who was in attendance.

The will of James Rodgers, dated August 7, 1926 (p. 180, Orphan's Court, Copiah County, Mississippi), names all of his and Elly's children except for one daughter. She is listed as the wife of William H. Wilson and is stated as deceased. In this book, I gave her the name of Sarah, the daughter killed by Indians. Her real name and the circumstances surrounding her death are unknown. Also, there was a twelfth child named Lavina, but in all of my research, I could not pinpoint when or where she was born, so I did not include her in the story.

If you have read the first book in the Okatibbee Creek series, *Okatibbee Creek*, you're familiar with its heroine, Mary Ann Rodgers. *Elly Hays* is the story of Mary Ann's paternal grandmother, Elizabeth Hays Rodgers, better known as Elly. If you have not read any of the Okatibbee Creek series, they are a collection of stories about one family and the strong women of our American past. These are the real-life stories of my grandmothers, aunts, and cousins, but if your family has long been in the United States, these stories could be about your female ancestors—the women who fought for us, for our safety, our lives, and our freedom, and who sacrificed everything with the depth of their love and astounding bravery.

Elizabeth "Elly" Hays Rodgers's legacy continues today, as her descendants number in the hundreds of thousands and have spread throughout the States. I know of descendants living in Mississippi, Alabama, Florida, Louisiana, Texas, California, North Carolina, Illinois, and Michigan. Elly's family continues under the surnames Rodgers, Matlock, Landrum, Phillips, Deaton, Kirk, Hendricks, Meek, Carpenter, and Jolly, to name a very few.

Many thanks go out to family, friends, and associates who provided invaluable support as this book was written:

Elyse Dinh-McCrillis: TheEditNinja.com
Jen Quist: JenQPhotography.com
Robert Hess: book designer

Elly Hays received honorable mention in general fiction at the 2013 Great Midwest Book Festival, it was named on the short list of "50 self-published books worth reading in 2013/14" at Indie Author Land, and the cover was named a semi-finalist at the 2014 Authorsdb Book Cover Contest. It also debuted as #1 on Amazon Kindle in Native American stories.

About the Author

Lori Crane was born in Meridian, Mississippi, and now lives in greater Nashville, Tennessee. She has been a life-long fan and student of genealogy after growing up without her father, and as the years passed, she became more and more obsessed with knowing everything possible about her roots. She became fascinated with the story of her fifth great grandmother Elizabeth "Elly" Hays Rodgers after writing two other books about the family, *Okatibbee Creek* and *An Orphan's Heart*. While writing about these strong heroines, she began to wonder where their strength came from, so she started backing up in time on the family tree.

Initially, she traced her roots back to Hays Rodgers, and through his service in the Mississippi Militia, she became a member of the United States Daughters of 1812. While studying the family and discovering what kind of lives the Rodgers family lived in that time period, she became convinced that Elly Hays was the beginning of the strong women in the family. However, there are undoubtedly others waiting to be discovered as Lori's journey continues.

Her line to Elly is: mother Linda Faye Culpepper Crane, grandfather Earl Wilmar Culpepper, great grandmother Annie Josephine Blanks Culpepper, second great grandmother Martha Lettie "Mattie" Carpenter Blanks, third great grandmother Mary Ann Rodgers Carpenter Jolly, fourth great grandparents Hays Rodgers and Marey A. Scott Rodgers, and fifth great grandparents James Rodgers and Elizabeth "Elly" Hays Rodgers.

Lori is also a member of the Daughters of the American Revolution, and the United Daughters of the Confederacy. She is a professional musician and member of the Screen Actors Guild-American Federation of Television and Radio Artists.

Please visit Lori's website
www.LoriCrane.com

Bibliography

Okatibbee Creek Series

Okatibbee Creek
An Orphan's Heart
Elly Hays

Stuckey's Bridge Trilogy

The Legend of Stuckey's Bridge
Stuckey's Legacy: The Legend Continues
Stuckey's Gold: The Curse of Lake Juzan

The Culpepper Saga

I, John Culpepper
John Culpepper the Merchant
John Culpepper, Esquire
Culpepper's Rebellion

Other Titles by Lori Crane

Savannah's Bluebird
Witch Dance
The Culpepper-Fairfax Scandal
On This Day: A Perpetual Calendar for Family
Genealogy

The following is an excerpt from

Okatibbee Creek

the first book in the Okatibbee Creek series

Okatibbee Creek

After an uneventful summer, a dismal harvest, and an empty, melancholy Christmas season, there is word that danger is brewing in the state of Mississippi. In January, we hear that General Sherman of the Union Army is heading east from Brandon on his way to destroy Meridian's railways, and he is bringing what appears to be the whole damn Union Army.

If his troops are marching toward Meridian, our little community stands right in his path. The rumors are that the Yankees are looting towns along their way. They are stealing food, horses, and livestock, and burning buildings, barns, cotton gins, and the unsold cotton bales that sit idle in the fields. They are looting homes, terrorizing residents, and taking whatever their rotten Yankee hearts desire. Then they are burning the homes down.

It has taken a long, long time, but finally the war is coming directly toward us. Unfortunately we have very few men left in town to fight the Yankees off.

We know we have to do something but we don't know what, so we meet at the church to come up with a plan.

One of the elderly men says, "We know the direction they will be coming from—the west side of our creek—so the first thing we need to do is burn down Perry Bridge. They won't be able to get to us without that bridge."

One of the other men nods in agreement. "Yes, they will have to go at least ten miles in either direction to cross that creek, and they're not going to waste time doing that if they're on their way to Meridian, so that will probably work."

We set out immediately, lay brush under the wooden bridge, and set it ablaze.

Our plan works. Our creek saves us. The Yankees stay on the west side of the creek and follow it south to Meridian. However, after they sack Meridian, they are apparently given orders to take the surrounding towns. They come back up on the east side of the creek, and this time they invade our little community in droves. There is absolutely nothing we can do to stop them, outside of joining the war effort and killing the scoundrels. They terrorize our residents. They burn down our barns. They invade our homes, looking for food and treasure.

I can hear Charlie screaming for me as he runs up the road. He flies in the front door of the store, shouting that the Union Army is coming down the street. Oh, no, here we go. Apparently I am now in the middle of this war. Unfortunately, on this day, I have all of the children with me: my three, William's four, and James's five.

I order the boys to run to the field in back and chase the hog and the horse into the woods. I order the girls to take every jug, every crock, and every jar of food from the store and the cellar, put them in the attic, barricade the door, and stay there. Then I load my rifle. I'll be damned if I'm going to let these disgraceful, plundering Yankees ruin my life any more than they already have. And I will kill every last one of them before I let them harm the children. When the Yankees arrive, I will be more than ready for them.

I watch for them out the front window of the store. My palms are sweating. My heart is pounding out of my chest. My breathing is heavy. I can also feel my anger rising like flames from the very depths of Hell. My hands are shaking, though I don't know if it is from fear or rage. I can hear them coming before I can see them. Their horses are clomping on the dry road and there is a jingling sound from their spurs and saddles. Sure enough, they stop right in front of my store. There are three of them on horseback dressed in their blue uniforms. They are filthy and unshaven and a bit thin and weary. I slowly emerge through the doorway onto the wooden front porch with my loaded rifle in my hands.

"What do you want?" I yell to the Yankees.

"Do you have any food here?" one of them asks, though it sounds more like a demand than a question.

"No, I don't have any food," I say, surprised at the sound of the strength in my own voice even though my statement is a bold lie.

"Is your husband home?" the second one asks.

"No. You already killed him," I reply, with venom in my tone that would scare off any other man, but they don't move.

"Is there a man of the house here?" the third one asks.

"No, there are no men here, just me." I raise my gun slightly.

"You need to put that gun away, ma'am. We just want some food. We're not here to hurt anyone. You have to have some kind of food in that store," the first one says with a cocky smile on his unshaven face, as he climbs down from his horse. He removes his dusty hat and takes a couple steps toward me.

"I already told you, I don't have any food," I say slowly without raising my voice. I do, however, raise my gun to my shoulder and point it squarely at the man's face. The two Yankees still on horseback put their hands on their pistols.

The man on the ground stops moving and holds up his free hand to the other two to keep them from drawing their weapons. Again, he starts to move toward me.

I cock the hammer. Again, he stops.

We seem to be at a stalemate. But what he doesn't know is that the rage inside me will have no trouble blowing his damn head off. We stare each other directly in the eye and neither of us moves.

Suddenly, there is a gunshot from behind the Yankees. All three of the men draw their weapons and spin around, but none of them know exactly which way to turn. My son Benjamin appears from around one corner of the store with a pistol pointing at the man in front of me. My nephew Allen John appears from around the other corner at the exact same time, with his rifle pointing at one of the men on horseback. Mr. Calhoun comes out from his hiding place behind a tree on the other side of the road, his rifle aimed at the second man on horseback. Mr. Pace appears from behind the shed next to the store, aiming at the man standing on the ground.

All of our guns are pointing directly at the

Yankees. They know they are surrounded and they don't like it one bit. It seems as if everyone freezes for a moment as the Yankees grasp their predicament.

The man on the ground, in a desperate move, quickly spins around and points his gun at me like he is trying to frighten me into dropping my gun.

William bursts through the doorway of the store behind me with his gun over my shoulder, aiming right at the Yankees' head.

"I wouldn't do that if I were you," William growls in a voice I have never heard before. "You boys need to move along now."

After a few moments that seem like an hour, the Yankee on the ground slowly holsters his gun, puts his hat back on his head, and lifts both hands in surrender as he backs up to his horse.

"We were just looking for something to eat. We didn't mean no harm," he stammers.

The men on horseback holster their weapons. None of us lower our weapons. None of us move. The man on the ground climbs back up on his horse, and the three of them ride off as fast as lightning.

After the men ride off, William reaches in front of me and takes the loaded rifle out of my trembling hands. I'm shaking and in shock. I stand frozen in sheer terror, thinking of what could have happened.

"Are you all right?" William asks softly.

"I don't know. I think so," I say, hearing the quiver in my voice.

I look up at him. "Why are you here?"

"Right place at the right time." He smiles.

William hands our weapons to Mr. Pace and Mr. Calhoun, who have joined us on the porch, and then he wraps his arms around me.

"It's all over. It's all over," he repeats as he holds me in his arms.

I start to cry. I'm not sure why. William holds me. He doesn't let go.

That evening, William and I hold vigil on the front porch, with a fire burning in the yard and our rifles loaded. We wait for the Yankees to return, but fortunately, they never do. While we sit and wait, we talk of the hard times we are all enduring, and of the war and what kind of future we might have.

William has a good farm, a lovely house, and four beautiful children. He says since three of his four children are girls and he is obviously short on boys to help with the farm, he is hoping the farm can be profitable enough so he can pay some laborers to help plant and harvest this coming year.

"Thank you for helping me with the children," he says. "Men can't raise babies. It's just not man's work. I didn't realize how much a man needs a woman to raise the children so he can work on the farm."

I say, "You're welcome." I don't reply to the rest of his statement. I know it is all true, but I don't know what he is going to do about it.

I rock in my chair as I look out across the field and admire the full moon and the stars. The silence of the night is only interrupted by the crickets and the occasional bullfrog croaking.

After a few minutes of silence between us, he asks, "Mary, why are you hanging on to this store?"

I try to think of an answer to give him. I feel a storm of grief well up inside of me as the reality of my situation hits me. I didn't realize until this moment that I keep myself busy to avoid thinking about it. I haven't allowed myself time to dwell on all that has happened or what the future might hold. Until now. Tears fill my eyes. I can't breathe for a moment. I try to compose myself so I can speak.

"This was Rice's dream. I tried my best to make it successful so when he returned from the war, he would be proud of me."

A sob catches in the back of my throat. I try not to cry, but tears come anyway. William sits quietly next to me and lets me work through my grief as the flood-gates open.

After a few minutes, the wave of grief passes and I take a deep breath.

I whisper through my tears, "He's not coming back."

The following is an excerpt from

An Orphan's Heart

the second book in the Okatibbee Creek
series

An Orphan's Heart

We stop in front of a quaint home with a white fence running all around the property. I can see by the light of the moon there are horses grazing in the pasture, and I can smell the fruit trees in bloom. The front of the house is lovely, with a long covered front porch that runs the length of the house. Willie grabs my bag from the back of the wagon and escorts me up the steps.

The front door flies opens, flooding the porch with light, and Mollie comes out to greet me, wiping her hands on a kitchen cloth. She's a beautiful woman with dark hair and green eyes. Even though she has sharp, chiseled features, she looks soft and approachable at the same time. She's wearing a dark gray dress with a faded yellow apron, and her hair is pulled neatly into a braid. Though Willie told me Mollie is twenty-five years old, she looks quite a bit older. I imagine since her mother became ill, she has not slept well.

"Ellen! Welcome! We're so happy you're here." She smiles and gives me a hug.

"Mollie, it's so nice to meet you, and I'm terribly

sorry about your mother."

She thanks me, then takes my arm and escorts me into the house.

The inside is as charming as the outside. A blazing fire warms the room, and the air smells of freshly made coffee. Mollie introduces me to their daughters: Minnie, who is five, and Willie Jo, who is two. What cute little girls! Judging by their nightdresses, they were about to go to bed. They both run up and wrap their arms around my neck as I bend down to say hello.

"Aunt Ellen, how long did it take you to get here?" Minnie asks.

"A couple of days. I traveled on three different trains."

"Did you bring us any presents?" Willie Jo asks.

I laugh. I didn't even consider doing so, but I pull two pieces of candy from my bag and they're happy with that.

I'm so wrapped up in the little girls, I don't even notice him sitting quietly at the table.

"Ellen, I'd like to introduce you to my brother. This is Sam Meek."

The man rises from the table to greet me, and I'm immediately taken aback by his rugged good looks and warm smile. Our eyes meet and lock. Suddenly I feel as if I'm drowning in a pool of green—the richest green of a mountainside, the darkest green of the deepest water. Everyone and everything else disappears.

He offers me his hand as I rise from the floor. "It's very nice to meet you."

"And you, sir." I take his hand and feel electricity flow through every vein in my body. I pull my hand away, and just as quickly regret the action. I wish to feel that sensation again, but there is no way to touch him again now. I glance down and admire his tan forearm, half covered by his rolled-up sleeve. "I am very sorry about the loss of your mother," I offer as I try to compose myself.

He doesn't respond for a moment, and stares deeply into my eyes. "Thank you. It's very sad for all of us." He doesn't pull his eyes away.

Mollie brings some coffee to the table, breaking the spell Sam Meek has created, and she motions for us to have a seat.

"Would you like something to eat?" she asks.

"No, thank you." I shake my head, finding it hard to look away from the exquisite creature in front of me.

"Sam?"

"No, I'm fine, but thank you," he says, not breaking our gaze. "I'll have to get to sleep in a little bit. I'm exhausted."

I sink into the chair but have no idea if I'm actually sitting. The thought of him leaving the room is disheartening, and I'm surprised a man I just met is having this kind of effect on me.

"So, how was your trip?" He turns toward his coffee cup as Mollie fills it.

"It was amazing. When I was younger, I traveled through a small town in Alabama that had a train station. I was so enchanted by the women in their fancy hats coming and going, I vowed to myself I would someday travel on a train to a distant place." I smile. "And here I am."

"Sounds nice." He takes a sip of his coffee, watching me over the brim of his steaming cup. His voice sounds like silk.

I watch the way he sips. I watch his strong, callused hands place the cup back down on the table. I watch his tongue lick a stray drop from his lips. I watch his tanned throat as he swallows.

"Did you sleep on the train or did you stop somewhere?"

"I spent the night in Mobile and New Orleans, but the rest of the trip was on a sleeper train that had bunks. The rocking motion of the train was actually very soothing." I sip the strong, bitter coffee, then glance at him as I place the cup back on the table.

"Well, I'm glad you had a good journey." He stands. "I'm sorry to interrupt our coffee and conversation, but I really need to get some sleep. I can hardly keep my eyes open. It's going to be a long day tomorrow with the funeral and all." He grabs his hat from the side table. "Relatives have been coming into town all day." He nods to me. "It was a pleasure to meet you, ma'am. I'd love to speak with you more about your journey, and I'll see you again tomorrow."

"Nice to meet you, too, Mr. Meek." His movements are like a stallion running through a field, like an eagle catching its prey, like a...

"Please, call me Sam." He grins, showing the slightest dimple under his dark stubble. His eyes sparkle in the firelight.

I nod and smile. I can't stop staring at him.

He bids a good evening to Mollie and Willie, and just as instantly as he appeared, he is gone.

My heart is pounding in my ears. My palms are sweating. I can't seem to catch my breath. I wish I could follow him. I look down at my coffee cup and shake my head. When I look up, Mollie and Willie are both staring at me, and I blush.

"Well," says Mollie, "you two seemed to have hit it off rather nicely. I'm glad you are here, Ellen." She smiles. "Sam was Momma's caretaker. Our father died four years ago, and Sam was the only one of us siblings who stayed here to look after her. He used to have quite a busy social life, but he put everything on hold for the last four years to take care of Momma. I'm sure he could use a friend. He's thirty, and he needs to get on with his life now." Mollie refills my coffee cup. "Are you sure you don't want something to eat?"

I shake my head and glance at the closed door, wishing Sam would come back into the room with the excuse that he forgot something.

The following is an excerpt from
The Legend of Stuckey's Bridge
the first in the Stuckey's Bridge Trilogy

The Legend of Stuckey's Bridge

1942, Lauderdale County, Mississippi

Billy yanked up on his fishing pole. His eight-year-old brother asked, "Did you catch somethin'?"

Billy frowned as he watched the tip of his pole arc. The line grew taut. "Naw, I think I'm just snagged," he grumbled.

"Oh, I though you got a catfish."

"I wish. I think I'm stuck on somethin'." He lifted his pole again, reeling in an inch or two of the line.

"Maybe you caught one of Old Man Stuckey's boots."

"Don't even say that, Bobby. It gives me the creeps."

The warm afternoon sun quickly disappeared behind ominous dark clouds, leaving the boys in an eerie dusk one usually witnesses just before nightfall.

Bobby looked up. "It's gonna rain. You better get that line in so we can go."

Billy looked up, too. A gust of wind caught the front wisp of his brown hair and gave him a chill.

"You know, everyone says he's still here," Bobby

snickered.

"Who?"

"Old Man Stuckey."

"Yeah, I know, but I'd rather not think about it. Besides, I'm a little busy at the moment." Billy wrinkled his forehead as he tugged on the line again, ever so slowly bringing it closer.

Bobby yelled into the air. "Old Man Stuckey, jump in there and unsnag that line." He giggled.

Billy didn't think it was funny and gave his younger brother a nasty look. "Don't call him," he whispered as if someone might hear him, even though he knew there wasn't a soul within miles of them.

Bobby rose from his seat on the bank, leaving his line dangling in the murky water. "Here, let me help you." He walked in front of Billy and reached out over the river, trying to grab the clear fishing line.

Billy lifted the pole into the air a third time, bending the tip. "Whatever it is, it's coming. It's just slow."

"Maybe it's the noose they hung him with." Bobby laughed.

Billy didn't.

The sunny afternoon was transforming into an oncoming storm, and the clouds were rolling in fast—gloomy, thick, menacing clouds. The breeze rustled Billy's hair again, making him shiver.

To the right of the young boys stood Stuckey's Bridge—a ninety-year-old bridge, one hundred twelve feet long, with a plank bottom and iron framework across the top. Some people fished from the top of the bridge, but Billy refused to step onto it. Bobby teased him incessantly about his fear of Old Man Stuckey's ghost, but Billy accepted the teasing and stayed firmly on the bank. The only reason he came out here at all was to catch the *big* catfish, and *they* lived under the bridge. As far as he knew, across the river stood nothing but trees and brush and the occasional woodland animal. In his twelve years of life, he never dared go across the bridge to see if there was more.

Bobby grabbed the line and took a step back, pulling it as he moved. "What the heck you got on here?"

When Bobby let go, Billy spun the reel, bringing in the line a foot or so. "I don't know, probably just a branch or some leaves from the bottom."

"Well, whatever it is, it's heavy." Bobby stepped forward to get another handful of the line.

A crow flew overhead, barely maintaining its airborne status in the strong gusts of wind. Billy looked up for a moment, thinking the crow to be a bad omen. His hands began to sweat on the cork handle of his fishing pole. He decided at that very moment it was time to go, and they both needed to bring their lines in quickly. "Bobby, I got it from here. You should pull in your line so we can get home. Looks like a big storm comin'."

Bobby looked up at the sky. "Yeah, okay." He let go of Billy's line and walked back over to his fishing spot. A quick movement on the other side of the river caught his eye. "What was that?"

"What was what?" said Billy, still concentrating on his line.

"Over there." Bobby pointed to the left across the river. "I saw somethin' in the trees."

Billy looked over but didn't see anything. "Probably a possum or somethin'." Then Billy heard something in the brush. He froze.

Bobby heard it, too. "I told you I saw somethin'. Maybe a bobcat?"

Thunder cracked like a cannon above the boys' heads and made them jump. Bobby grabbed his pole and frantically reeled his line in. It was quickly growing dark and the wind was increasingly stronger. He watched Billy pull and tug at the line.

"It's almost free," Billy assured him. "It's comin' faster."

Bobby looked at the other side of the river. "Dang! There it is again. There's somethin' over there all right."

Billy glanced across the river, but with the dimming light, he couldn't see anything even if it was there. He pulled his line harder. A twig snapped across the river. Both boys darted their gazes in that direction but saw nothing but darkening woods.

"Maybe it's him!" Bobby teased.

"Stop it! Don't be stupid, Bobby."

Billy slowly but deliberately reeled in the line. He pointed the tip of his pole toward the water to keep it from snapping with the weight of the mystery catch, and he kept turning the reel. A drop of rain fell on his forehead, mingled with the nervous sweat on his brow, and gave him another shiver.

"Hurry up, Billy. We're gonna get soaked."

"I am hurrying. I don't want to break my line."

The crow sounded loudly from across the river, and shot straight up above the tree line as fast as an arrow released from a bow. The boys looked that way, knowing something was in the woods, just out of sight. Another branch snapped.

"What the heck is that?" Bobby sounded nervous,

staring into the encroaching darkness on the other side of the river.

Billy didn't answer. He was absorbed in the blob he was dragging across the top of the murky water.

Bobby looked out at the greenish-brown blob. "You got nothin' but leaves. Let's go."

Billy pulled the blob onto the edge of the bank and laid his pole on the ground. He moved toward the blob to dislodge his hook, and noticed something shining in the blob. *What is that? It's shimmering. What the...?*

Another branch snapped across the river.

"Come on, Billy. We gotta go. Now."

"Hold on," Billy said as he grabbed a stick and poked into the blob, separating the leaves and muck.

Yes, there was something shiny. *Something gold.*

Thunder rumbled. A rustling sound came from across the river, making Bobby look in that direction again. Heavy, fat raindrops splattered on their heads, and dead leaves began to whirl around the banks of the river in the increasing winds. *It's something round.* The crow cawed noisily. Another twig snapped. *It's a watch.* Thunder roared again. *On a gold chain.* Lightning lit the sky in a jagged pulse for a few short seconds. The wind intensified.

"What is that?" Bobby asked.

"It's a pocket watch." Billy reached down and rubbed the mud off the front of the watch. He cocked his head to the side and saw a single T embossed in the gold. Simultaneously, the thunder roared, the crow cawed, the rustle across the river grew louder, and to their right, a giant splash scared both boys into standing straight up.

They stared, mouths agape, in the direction of the

bridge. Right under it, the water rippled in a circle as if something very, very large had just been dropped off the bridge. Thunder rumbled again. The water rippled more. The boys froze. An inch above the water in the center of the ripple was an eerie green glow. Instead of dissipating as they expanded, the ripples seemed to grow larger and higher in the ever-growing circle, as if the ocean tide was causing waves to come ashore.

The boys didn't look at each other. They didn't communicate. They turned at the same time and ran away as fast as their feet would carry them. They didn't grab their fishing poles. They didn't look back.

Lightning flashed while raindrops splattered the rocks, turning them from gray to brown. As the storm strengthened, the ripples inched up onto the bank, and little by little, pulled the gold pocket watch back into the murky depths.

www.ingramcontent.com/pod-product-compliance
Lightning Source LLC
Chambersburg PA
CBHW061142170626
46809CB00003B/962